Spare Hearts

Dorothy F. Shaw

T. D. Hoffman

Red Queen
Publications

Praise for Dorothy F. Shaw

"It was hysterical, charming and H-O-T!!! The dialogue between Sterling and Candy is incredibly well written, full of southern twang. The love scenes are intense and scorchingly sexy. Even the secondary characters are a hoot...especially Trudie. Definitely check this out if you like a very spicy romance with a down-home charm."—Harlequin Junkies on *Spare Hearts*

"Candy and Sterling are great characters with a lot of depth and a few hang-ups. The sexy scenes are fan-worthy, especially that first one, which I won't give away because it's awesome."—Jazzie book reviews on *Spare Hearts*

"*Unworthy Heart* reminded me of what I love about the romance genre."—The Book Tart

"*Unworthy Heart* by Dorothy F. Shaw made me think, made my heart happy, made me tear up and made me sigh in happiness. Shaw combines heat with heart almost flawlessly. I cannot wait for the follow-up books in this series."—Romance Novel News

troubles in their path."—Amazon reviewer on *Avoiding the Badge*

"I liked this book, I fell in love with Derek."—Heather - A Crazy Vermonter's Book Reviews on *Avoiding the Badge*

"*Redeeming the Badge* is second chance romance that is hot as Hades and with a backstory that will twist your heartstrings." —Amazon Reviewer

"This is a tale of love, and heartache, dealing with some tough issues such as infertility, endometriosis, and miscarriage. It will tear at your heartstrings, and make you believe in true love." —Amazon Reviewer on *Redeeming the Badge*

"Jeff and Tish are good couple with incredible chemistry that makes you jealous. I can't recommend this Series enough." — Amazon Reviewer on *Trusting the Badge*

"*Trusting the Badge* is a quick read for readers who enjoy a focus on relationship building, characters with tragic backstories, and some steamy moments." —Amazon Reviewer

"It was written in a way that I got very emotional reading it, most books don't make me cry. This one did."—Amazon reviewer on *Jaded Heart*

"As usual, Shaw creates characters that can be hard to like. Garrett is not easy to connect to. He treats Angie like crap, but Angie keeps fighting for them. Their flameout moment is painful to read about but very necessary. Garrett has to deal with his past, which he has been avoiding for years and years. With all of this, I still couldn't put the book down."— Romance Novel News on *Jaded Heart*

Spare Hearts

Candy Jameson has been stuck in this dead-end Texas town for way too long—and she's craving a little excitement. Enter Sterling Day: smoldering, confident, and just what she needs to shake things up… if only for a night.

But their fiery chemistry quickly turns into something more, and suddenly, one night doesn't feel like enough. Candy's not sure she's ready to risk her heart, especially on a guy just passing through.

Sterling, a former pro bowler chasing a comeback, came to this quiet town to focus. The last thing he expected was the irresistible night manager with a sharp tongue and curves that won't quit.

As passion deepens and the stakes rise, Candy and Sterling will have to decide—are they just playing the lanes, or is this the real thing?

Dedication

When plotting this story, we couldn't resist using the name of a very dear friend of mine who passed in 2012.

Sterling would have loved that we used his name for our adorable pro-bowler.

This one is for you, Sterling. You are missed, my friend.
Love, Dorothy

For Sterling
RIP 01/04/12

His Journey

The velvet night sky stretches wide
A lonely canvas painted by clouded memories
Love eagerly seeks a place
Away from the brewing storm
To rest his weary soul

A Heart sings a call above frigid winds
Beyond creation it waits
With limitless calm and patience
For Love to find his way
Back home

Thunder crashes
Lightning brightens the darkened sky
The Heart's song penetrates the deafening rain
Its chorus woven and complete
Fueled with adoring passion and simple melody

Love hears the Heart's call
Rising above the mutiny
He launches and soars beyond winds high

His delicate spirit touches and ignites the stars
Then winks at the moon as he travels by

He knows the Heart promises reprieve
Warmth and peace
The Heart swells and beats in anticipation
As finally Love settles before it

His journey is over
Love has found his place
The heart cradles him
Within its arms
Soothing Love's tired soul

He sleeps

—Dorothy F. Shaw

Acknowledgments

From both

Jennifer Sylvia, Christa Desir and Louisa Baccio for their excellent editing skills and willingness to kick our butts in order to get this book ready for submission.

Megan Hart, Crystal Posey and Wendi Cristner for their author eyes, much-needed feedback and constant encouragement.

All our wonderful beta readers: Barbi, Marchelle, Lu, Allison, Charlene, Adrienne and Holly.

Love, appreciation and thanks to all of you. We couldn't have done this without you.

From Dorothy

To my ex-husband, T.D.–AKA Wookie. Thank you for seeing Sterling so clearly in your mind and writing this fun story with me. To Carrie Clevenger, an incredible author, for inspiring my first poem and then pushing me to keep writing! Thank you for being my inspiration.

From T.D.

Special thanks to my high school English teacher, Mrs. White, for encouraging me to share my stories and my parents for teaching me to believe I can do anything.

Note to readers

As I've received my publishing rights back to this book, it's important to note that this is a re-released version. The title is the same, but the cover is different.

I also did a run-through of the entire book and did a little editing, a little updating and a little tweaking here and there. Really, I just polished it all up.

So, now that that's clear, I wanted to take a quick moment to give you all a little history about this story.

Though Spare Hearts was not the first book I ever wrote (it was the second, actually), it was the first book I was lucky enough to have published.

And that makes it pretty special to me. I also had the privilege to write it with my now ex-husband, Wookie.

Now, you might wonder…why a book about a pro-bowler? Bowlers aren't hot, are they?

To this, I say that while I'm sure there are many very good-looking and sexy bowlers, pro or not, out there in the world, I know for sure that in the wonderful world of romance books, a pro bowler can be as sexy as we want him to be.

That said, there's a little story behind how this hot bowling hero book came to be.

Lauren Plude was a young editor working with Hachette-Grand Central Publishing House, and at that time, she was bowling in a league with friends.

In the good old days of Twitter, she tweeted about this quite a lot and also tweeted that she wanted more submissions of books with sports heroes in them.

I saw that tweet (as well as the others) and replied to her that the fact that she was bowling on a league made me want to write a hot bowling hero for her.

She replied (mind you, she didn't know me), saying, YES! Please write me a bowling hero!

Wasting no time, I started plotting.

When my husband (now my ex) came home from work, I told him I wanted to write a book with a hot bowling hero.

He laughed and said, you mean like the movie "Kingpin?"

Of course, I was said, definitely NOT like "Kingpin."

Anyway, he started plotting with me, and we got pretty far into it. As the story unfolded, I asked him to write it with me. He was also an aspiring writer, so he agreed.

We honestly had a blast writing this book. We laughed pretty much throughout the entire thing! We especially laughed at the different southern colloquialisms we used in the story.

Strawn, Texas, is an actual place, and all the restaurants listed in the book, at the time it was written, were actual places of business, too.

The only thing that wasn't real was the bowling alley, Bowling Dreams. But that's the fun of writing fiction. You get to take some creative license where it makes sense and add things that don't exist.

And then, deciding on the hero's name came easy. Sterling Day was a friend of mine who we lost far too young. As I said in my dedication to him, he would've found this whole thing hilarious. In our original version, we had changed the spelling of his last name primarily because we weren't sure if his family would be okay with us using it.

But, after the book was released, we discovered they were fine with it. Sterling's mother (who is a saint, in my opinion) was so honored and excited that we used her beloved son's name and dedicated the book to him that she often promoted it on her social media to her friends.

With that in mind, since I'm re-releasing the book after getting the rights back, I decided to update Sterling's last name to the correct spelling of "Day" instead of the initial spelling we used of "Dey."

All that said, I hope you enjoy Sterling and Candy.

Their story is meant to be campy, cute and naughty. Trudie is my absolute favorite character, but that's because I'm old, and Flo was the bomb when I was a kid.

(If you're over 50, you know who Flo is. If not, all I have to say is, "Kiss my grits!" 😄)

Remember, the best compliment you can give an author is a review. But…it's also word of mouth. So, as my good friend, author Megan Hart, always says: "If you like it, tell everyone you know to read it. If you hate it, tell everyone you *hate* to read it."

Love, Dorothy!

Chapter One

CANDY PEERED up from her crouched position behind the blue laminate counter to see Toby Hansen leaning over the top, staring down her shirt. Again.

"Howdy, Candy."

"Hey, Toby." She sighed, finished putting away the disinfectant spray, and stood. "You needin' somethin'?"

"My, you look pretty tonight." Toby leered, displaying the large gap between his front teeth.

"Aww, you're so sweet." Candy plastered a practiced smile on her face and stifled the shudder running through her body.

Toby straightened and popped both thumbs in his front pockets. "Shucks, fine as you are, you make it easy to be sweet." He laughed, causing his large belly to shake and slip from under his shirt.

"Stop that now. You'll make me blush." She waved her hand at him. "What'd you need?"

He eyed her cleavage again, and she cleared her throat in order to pull his attention back to her face.

Most men were raised right and proper and didn't gawk like Toby was doing—or at least they weren't so obvious about it.

Candy wasn't afraid to show her body off. Didn't mind the attention either. But there was a difference between looking and downright rude staring.

"Oh, uh…ball's stuck on six." He continued to stare at her chest.

"Again? That dang thing. Let me give a holler back to Joe and get you taken care of." She grabbed the ancient house phone to ring the pinsetter area, praying Toby wouldn't tell her all the ways he'd like her to take care of him.

Toby winked at her, then stepped away from the counter.

Thank the Lord above for small miracles. It might've been over two years since she'd seen any action between the sheets, but she sure as heck wasn't desperate enough to take the likes of Toby Hansen into her bed.

If she had to hear him go on again, like last Friday night, about her "perky assets," she might just vomit right there on all the bowling shoes she'd finished disinfecting.

She leaned against the counter, phone to her ear, and waited for Joe to pick up. "Dammit, that hick never answers," she muttered and hung up.

Candy walked from the front desk and headed for the area behind the pinsetting machines. The worn heels of her pink cowgirl boots clicked on the concrete floor as she made her way down the small walkway at the end of the fifteen lanes.

She hated going back there. Dingy old machines creaked as they loaded and reloaded pins, and the loud crack of the ball, as it connected with its target, made her ears ring.

She'd probably find Joe snoozing, boots kicked up, hat covering his face. Good God, sometimes she hated this job almost as much as she hated this mom-and-pop town she was stuck in. The job paid the bills, though, so complaining was a waste of brain cells.

Candy always thought she'd be happily married with kids at this age or maybe have some sort of career. She'd done the married thing but missed the happily and the kids parts by a long shot. And the alley sure as heck wasn't a career.

Divorced and twenty-eight years old. And she still hadn't dug her way out.

Someday it's gonna happen.

THIS DRIVING CRAP was for the birds.

In the past, when Sterling had his "pro" status, he'd flown to all the tournaments. Now, no such luck. It was proving to be a long, hard road back to the championships…and better travel arrangements.

His desire to win, his need to prove to himself he could still do it after all this time, and his stubbornness were exactly what had led him to the here and now.

Now being on his way to Strawn, Texas, a one-horse town, to spend a month focusing on his game before the big tournament in Fort Worth and, hopefully, his life-changing moment.

Sterling took a deep breath as he exited the highway and was faced with a giant billboard.

Welcome to Strawn, Texas.
Home of The National Bowling Champion
Mason Jennings

Damn, they sure are proud of their hometown hero.

Sterling swore every tiny town *had* to have its claim to fame.

His manager, Troy, had convinced him this place was exactly what he needed to focus and make sure he was bringing his A-Game to the tourney. Less distraction, Tony had said.

Apparently, Troy was old friends with the town's bowling alley owner and called in a favor. For Sterling, it was just another stop on the way to getting his life back.

Plus, he liked to keep a low profile, anyway. Who needed all the sports writers chasing you down and snapping pictures at all the wrong times? He sighed. *I do. That's who.*

A bright orange vacancy sign flickered on the side of the two-lane main road. Sterling slowed to pull into the hotel parking lot, but when he saw the giant flashing **BOWLING DREAMS** sign on the building next door, he lifted his foot off the brake, coasted forward, and parked there instead.

Dreams, huh? How appropriate.

The brisk night air whipped across his skin when he swung the truck door open. The coolness slapped him in the face and chased off any remaining drowsiness.

He pulled himself out of the driver's seat and stretched the fatigue from his legs. Twisting his waist until he felt—and heard—a loud crack that loosened his spine, he let out a sigh of relief.

Sterling smoothed out his jeans and leaned inside the F-150 to retrieve his favorite cowboy hat before crossing the parking lot to check in to the hotel.

It was more of a "motel," really. A couple dozen doors on the front of a single-story brick building faced the parking lot. He would move his truck later when he found out which room was his.

After completing the long check-in process, Sterling turned back for the door and ran his thumb over the plastic diamond-shaped key chain and room key.

What has Troy gotten me into? When was the last time he checked in to a motel that still used actual keys?

Shoving the key in his pocket, Sterling returned to his truck and, after retrieving his bowling bag from the covered bed, headed for the double-door glass entry of Bowling Dreams. "Might as well check the place out."

4

He eyed the inside of the alley; a grand total of three, maybe four, people were in the whole building. *Gee, I wonder if I can get a lane.*

At the empty front counter, he set his bag on the floor and grabbed a sucker out of his shirt pocket. Pulling the wax paper off, he looked for somebody, anybody who might be working tonight.

He popped the hard candy into his mouth, root beer flavored, his favorite. Leaning his body against the counter, he began tapping the championship ring he wore on his right hand against the laminate top.

CANDY LEANED OVER A SNORING JOE.

"Hey! Wake up!" She flipped the hat off his head and stepped back as he jumped out of his skin, his eyes scanning the space wildly.

"Dammit, Candy. Hate it when you do that." He spat a mouthful of tobacco juice on the floor and got to his feet.

"Ugh, gross! Hate it when you do *that.*" She held back an urge to gag. "If you'd keep your 'hind awake, I wouldn't have to scare the tar outta you." She spun on her heel.

"What'd you need, anyway?"

Shoot, she'd almost forgot. "Ball stuck on six!" she yelled over her shoulder, exiting as fast as she'd come in.

With hands tucked in the back pockets of her cutoff denim shorts, Candy wandered back down the narrow walk. At least the music was good on Friday nights, compared to the rest of the week, though the crowd had been getting pretty dang thin on the weekends.

With the economy the way it was, it made her worry she'd have to find a way out of Strawn sooner than she could afford.

As she approached the front desk, she couldn't help noticing the tall, cool drink of water leaning against the counter. *Sweet Jesus, who is that?* Candy took in his lean form as she got closer: Standard-issue cowboy boots, long legs covered in nice-fitting jeans that hugged a back end, just begging to be grabbed.

Candy's sleeping libido woke up and took notice. This man, for sure, did *not* live around here. If she could just see his—

She stopped short as she rounded the corner of the counter.

My God, he had the prettiest blue eyes she'd ever seen. High cheekbones and lush lips framed by a close-trimmed beard. All topped by a black cowboy hat.

Candy swallowed past the lump forming in her throat and focused on the front of his royal blue button-down shirt, trying for all it was worth to calm the pitter-patter of her heart. The way his broad chest filled out the fabric sent a wave of lust barreling through her.

For Lord's sake, she needed to keep it together long enough to greet a new customer.

"Howdy." He pulled the lollipop from his mouth. "Is Mason Jennings available?" He smiled, displaying his near-perfect teeth.

"Not at this hour. He usually works the day shift." She shook herself and forced her eyes away from his mouth.

"Dang. Should've figured."

"Is there anythin' I can help you with?" She brushed her thick hair off her shoulder.

He raised his arm to glance at his watch, and the muscle in his bicep bunched, tightening his shirtsleeve with the movement. "Any chance of gettin' a lane tonight?"

"Of course." Dragging her eyes back to his, she settled her fingers on the keyboard to check him in. "Welcome to Bowling Dreams. Will you be needin' shoes?"

Suddenly thirsty, Candy was surprised she managed to speak without sounding like she had a mouth full of cotton.

"No, ma'am, I have my own." He tapped his ring on the counter.

Candy activated his lane on the register system and reached for her water bottle under the counter. "You can take ten. Right there across from the counter."

"Thank you kindly." He tipped his hat, popped the lollipop between his lips, and turned away.

"Let me know if you need anything." *Anything. Really, please don't hesitate to ask.*

"Will do." He grinned over his shoulder.

She laughed and rested her elbows on the counter, watching him walk away. Dang fine view she had of his hind end. Butterflies swarmed in her tummy at the sight, and her cheeks got hot. Actually, she was hot all over.

Ten was the perfect choice, and she thanked the Lord it had been available. Now she could watch him and hopefully not drool all over herself until closing from her station.

Candy may not have found her way out of Strawn yet, but at least she had something fine to pay attention to while she passed the time tonight.

Chapter Two

SETTING his bag down and taking a seat, Sterling had almost forgotten the one major attraction of small towns: small-town girls.

Sure, he was tired. Sure, he needed to focus on the big picture. But damn if a beautiful girl didn't help serve as a nice distraction.

He unzipped his bag and pulled out his custom-made bowling shoes. He toed off his boots, tucked them under the chair, and laced up his signature flashy royal blue and silver best friends.

Crunching on the tail end of his sucker, he grabbed his personalized ball out of his bag and snuck a glance back at the counter girl. *Damn,* if she wasn't purty as all get-out.

A set of pouty full lips glistening with lip gloss, a straight nose turned up just at the tip, and a head full of the thickest dirty blonde hair he'd ever seen. He bet all that hair would look sexy as hell draped across his chest.

Sterling loved petite women, and looking just under five feet tall, this girl had his attention. *Focus, man!*

After depositing his ball in the return tray, he turned to

Dorothy F. Shaw & T. D. Hoffman

walk back to enter his name in the score computer and caught her staring. Sterling's curiosity piqued. *Well, I'll be...*

Maybe he caught her attention, too. "Ya know, you never did introduce yourself."

The slight crimson flush washing across her high cheeks let him know she'd heard him speaking to her. She walked around from behind the counter, and Sterling wasn't the least bit disappointed by the view he got.

A pink and gray plaid button-up shirt tied into a halter top displaying a generous amount of cleavage, a narrow waist flowing into a pair of tiny little cutoff denim shorts framing a nice full set of hips. Damn, curvy in all the right places.

"I think you're right. I'm Candy Jameson. Sorry 'bout that." A smile looking like it'd jumped off a Victoria's Secret catalog adorned her lips. "Kitchen's closed this late, but I might be able to rustle up somethin' for you. You look... hungry." She winked.

Suddenly famished, Sterling hoped she might offer to be the main course.

"Candy, huh? That's sweet. I like it. Name's Sterling Day." He reached in his bag for his wrist brace and let his gaze linger over her as he fitted it to his right arm. "How 'bout a coke?"

"We have a full bar if you want somethin' harder, hon."

"Nah, no alcohol for me, coke's good." He grabbed another one of his suckers, unwrapped it, and held it up, waving it to tease her. "I like candy more."

Her eyes lit up, and she draped her hair over one shoulder, running her fingers through the thick tresses. "What kind?"

"Regular coke'll do just fine."

"Comin' right up." She smiled. "I'll be right back."

Sterling's eyes waved from side to side, and his breath hitched as he tracked the hypnotic rhythm of her plentiful hips. Her backside taunted him, and arousal rocketed through

10

him hard and fast while watching her sashay her way to the bar. *Bowl, ya damn hick. Gonna go pro again, remember?*

Shaking his head to wrangle his thoughts, he put his hat on the seat and walked over to the ball return. *Focus. Get in the game.*

With his routine planted in his mind, he gathered his ball and polished off any possible oil residue with his towel. Staring down the thin boards, he locked his eyes on the pins and declared to himself they would all fall.

Sterling let his fingers hover over the hand dryer, then slid them into his ball; the holes fit perfectly. Of course, they did— the thing had been custom-made for him and was the same one he won the championship with all those years ago.

He dropped his towel on the rack and started toward the far right side of the lane to line up his target. The countdown had begun. One month until his big return to the game. It was his last chance as far as he was concerned.

It was rare that anyone tried for a second shot at the pros. Life for him had never been the same since, and he wanted— no, he needed—the thrill of the win again.

He extended his arms in front of him and lowered his eyes to lock on his target: the arrows halfway up the bed and two boards in from the edge.

He stepped toward the foul line and swung his arm back, bringing the ball high above his shoulder. His arm descended as gravity took hold of the weight; he added his muscle to the arc of his wrist and released the ball in a whirlwind of spin.

The flamboyant silver and blue swirled blur took off in a straight line, taunting the edge of the gutter before a wicked curve to the left on course for his target took over.

Sterling held his pose until the sound he lived for echoed in his ears, the splintering ricochet of the pins exploding into the pit when his ball connected in the pocket. Strike!

"Nice form. You look like you mighta' done this a time or two."

As he walked back toward the ball return, Candy's melodic voice drifted into his ear, snapping his attention to her as every hair on his body stood on end.

Damn, if her voice didn't cut right through the din of the pins resetting.

Chapter Three

CANDY WATCHED in awe as Sterling rolled through his motions.

His approach and release showed a level of skill she'd never seen in the alley before. The owner's father was a former PBA champ, but she'd never seen him bowl.

Sterling's seriousness made her laugh, though. Bowlers were so intense! She wondered if he was like that all the time. Candy enjoyed bowling but tried to be more lighthearted and fun about the game.

Either way, when that ball struck home over and over and all pins scattered as if in fear for their lives, she knew Sterling had to be something special.

He cocked his head to the side, holding the towel in his hand. "Thanks. You could say I've spent some time in the lanes."

Sterling scooped up the ball from the return and spun it in the towel.

"I guess so. That's one heck of a curve you got there." She stepped closer and took the chance to get a better glimpse of his short, salt-and-pepper hair. *Wonder if it's as soft as it looks.*

"Here's your coke." She placed the beverage on the half wall separating the bowling floor from the main area. "I'm just a holler away if you decide you're wantin' somethin' else." She stuffed her hands in her back pockets and looked up and down his tall body, enjoying the view. *Good Lord, stop gawkin' at the dude. Go back to the counter, Candy.*

"Much obliged, ma'am." He turned back to the pins for his next shot.

With his back turned, she made a quick getaway back behind the counter, where she could watch him. And his fine butt. His long legs. And his— *Jeezus, stoppit!*

For the first time in...well, she didn't know how long; she was happy the lanes were empty tonight. It meant she wouldn't have to take her eyes off him for long, if at all.

She grabbed the stool behind the counter, straddled it, and watched him throw ball after ball down the maple and pine boards.

Near every ball made a strike. When it didn't, Sterling changed position and picked up the spare. Lordy, the man rolled like a pro. But he sure looked different from any pros she'd seen on TV.

Sterling Day—*what a cool name*—was easy on the eyes. To be honest, how many bowlers were *actually* good-looking? Especially the ones around here? And the pro bowlers? Forget it.

But this cowboy was swoon-worthy, for sure. He had skill. Looked like *real* skill, too. It made him all the more appetizing to her.

Could there be a sexier man out there? *He sure does like them lollipops. Betcha I'm sweeter, cowboy.*

With both elbows propped on the counter and her chin resting on her hands, Candy imagined how strong he might be and if all that power he pushed down the lane worked in the bedroom, too.

Her skin prickled with goose bumps, and butterflies fluttered in her tummy at the thought of him giving *her* a spin with the impressive wrist skill he showed off. *What would it take to get him in my bed?*

"You look like you're havin' one helluva daydream, darlin'," a voice with a familiar Texas twang said, interrupting that daydream.

Candy glanced over at her friend. Never a hair out of place, and her makeup was always perfect, though she wore a ton of it. The woman could make Mary Kay herself proud. It was like seeing Flo, who worked at Mel's Diner in the old TV show Alice, but with bleached white-blonde hair.

Candy adored her, eccentricities and all.

"Take a gander over there." Candy motioned with her chin toward Sterling.

"Howw-dyy. Who is that, and can I have a taste of his lean muscles?" Trudie's orange-lipsticked lips spread into a grin.

"No kiddin'. He looks all strong and lickable."

"Tall, too." Trudie propped a hip against the counter and sighed. "But too young for me."

They both stood there for a few minutes, taking in their fill of the new stud in town, until Trudie broke the silence again. "He's one hell of a cranker."

"Were you needin' something?" Candy asked.

"Oh, hell. Tall, cool and delicious—like I like my gin and tonics—distracted me. I need some singles." She handed Candy two twenty-dollar bills and a ten.

"No problem." Candy opened the register drawer, pulled out a wrapped bundle of fifty ones, and handed them to Trudie. "How many you got in there tonight?"

"The usual pickled good 'ol boys and a few gray-haired ladies from town." Trudie rolled her eyes. "Friday night excitement in Strawn, Texas, and Bowling Dreams is the *hippest* place to be." She batted her thick lashes, then fluffed her bleached white head of hair.

"You realize how scary that is, right?"

"Sure do." Trudie strolled out from behind the counter and made her way back to the bar.

Now, where was I? Candy focused her attention back on the best distraction she'd had in forever and watched as he rubbed his shoulder.

"You look like a man on a mission." Candy moved around the counter and approached him. "I got ice in the back for your shoulder. If you want."

"Thank ya kindly." He ran his palm over his shoulder again. "I can't help but wonder if a little heat might be more up my alley."

"I think we have one of those instant heat packs in the office. You want me to check?"

"I may take you up on that later if it keeps up. Thanks." Sterling leaned against the half wall and crossed his arms over his very broad chest.

Shifting her weight to one foot, Candy rested her hand on her hip. "You throw one heck of a ball. You ever think of goin' pro?"

"Think about it? Already done it." He raised his hand, flashing her his champion ring, then removed his hat and swiped his palm over the top of his short hair before setting it back in place. "Planning on doin' it again, too."

"I knew you had too much talent for just any cowboy." She tugged on the tails of her halter top and rolled to the balls of her feet as excitement pulsed through her. "That shoulder the reason you stopped, I'm guessin'?"

"Yup, damn fool injury took me out of the game for a while. Plannin' on changing that, though."

"Well, you're lookin' good from my angle." She raised her hand and pointed at him. "Hey, wait! There's a national tourney in Fort Worth next month, isn't there?"

"That's where I'm headin'. Gotta admit, I'm feelin' real good about the way I'm knockin' down the pins tonight." He pulled another sucker from his bag. "Should be one heck of a ride."

"Maybe you needed a little lucky charm to show off for." She batted her eyes at him. My Lord, did that just come out of her mouth?

"Maybe so." He set his sucker, still in its wrapper, next to his glass. "Or maybe I need better candy."

"Well, Sterling, I happen to know for a *fact* that Strawn has the best candy around for miles." She raised a brow and pursed her lips.

Candy couldn't believe she was flirting like this with him. But she didn't want to stop, either. It was fun to cut loose with a guy for a change. "I'm gonna be closin' up soon. You wanna practice awhile longer?"

"I think I'd like that, darlin'." He took a sip of his coke. "Don't want to get you in any trouble, though."

"I think I can keep the lanes open for you. Maybe I'll even join you for a game." She picked up his sucker from the ledge. "If I play with you tonight, you won't be needin' this."

Sweet baby Jesus, what was she doing? Turning, she moved back to the counter.

Candy never came on to men like she'd done with Sterling. Her hormones were taking over, ignoring all sense and reason, and before she knew it, she was flirting like a mare in heat.

With a deep breath, she looked down at the lollipop she'd taken from him in her hand and pushed away any nervousness rolling around her tummy.

He obviously didn't mind, and if she let herself think on it any longer, she'd end up making some weak excuse about why she couldn't stay open late for him.

Candy had been in high school when she met her ex-husband, and she'd had sex only once with one other person before Jared and none after.

She'd had plenty of offers in the last couple of years since her ex left, but she hadn't been interested in any of the guys in town. In truth, Jared had done such a number on her she didn't trust her judgment when men were concerned anymore.

But Sterling sparked a fire inside her with his fine body and pretty blue eyes; to top it off, he was polite, too.

A long-missed throb pulsed between Candy's thighs, and her nipples tightened inside her bra. It'd been well over two years since she'd gotten laid, and no one needed to know, and no one *would* know.

The last thing she wanted was for everyone in this godforsaken small town knowing she'd given it up to some traveling pro bowler.

She had enough of a reputation with Jared and his antics before he skipped town, leaving her high and dry as it was.

She needed this, and why the heck not, right? He'd be gone before anyone was the wiser, and she deserved a little roll in the hay.

Fine as all get out, and not from around there? *I think Sterling Day needs to make* my *day. I'm goin' for it.*

Chapter Four

CANDY CASHED out the remaining customers, ignored the typical sleazy compliments from Toby, and then counted out her and Trudie's cash drawers.

She looked around for Sterling and realized he'd probably headed to the men's room, maybe hiding out until everyone had left. *Smart man.*

Joe and Trudie came over to walk out with her.

"I guess tall, cool and delicious took off?" Trudie shouldered her large designer knockoff purse.

"Sure did. Was fun watchin' him, though. Lord have mercy, I could stand a bit more of that." Candy fanned herself.

She told them both to go on without her, explaining she had some paperwork to attend to in the back office and would take a while—nothing out of the ordinary, being the night manager and all.

"Tall, cool and delicious?" Joe snorted.

"Never you mind." Trudie hooked her arm in Joe's. "Don't stay too late, sweetheart. You need your beauty rest."

"I won't. Night, y'all." She locked the front doors after they both walked out.

With no sign of Sterling still, she grabbed her purse from beneath the counter and ran into the little quarter bathroom in the office behind the front desk.

She needed to check her hair and makeup. Lord only knew how she looked. If she was a mess, he'd already seen it, though.

Shaking her head at her silliness, she applied a little more lip gloss and adjusted her breasts in her push-up bra.

Not that the girls needed to be any higher on her chest, but she guessed every little bit helped when you were looking to get a man naked.

"You still here?"

She poked her head out. "In the office, be right there." She grabbed her bowling bag and made her way out to the front counter. "You ready to play that game with me?"

He arched one brow. "Sweetheart, we can do whatever you want."

"Whatever I want, huh?" She made her way around the counter. "Set 'em up, cowboy. I may just kick your ass." Giggling, she sauntered toward the lane.

"I might enjoy that." Sterling followed her as far as the score machine, stopping to sit at the computer and set up the game.

After Candy put on her bowling shoes, she set her ball in the tray and then spun around. "You're not married, are you? Because if you are—"

"Hell no, I'm not married."

"Good, me either." She placed her hand over her heart as relief washed over her. She was no home wrecker.

"With all that flirtin', it's a little late to be asking me now, don't ya think?"

"Oh, Lord!" Candy covered her mouth with her hand, attempting to stifle a laugh. How embarrassing. He was right —it *was* a little late to be asking now.

He got up and stepped in front of her. "Don't ever cover

that perfect smile of yours." He pulled her hand away from her mouth.

Heat crept its way up her chest, and her face got hot.

He stood so close she could smell his cologne mixed with a hint of clean soap. Pleasing and not too strong. She took a deep breath and looked up into his cornflower-blue eyes.

"I believe you're up, beautiful." He tapped the tip of her nose with his finger.

"You sure you're ready?"

"Bring it on, as they say." He took a seat.

Nervous energy carried Candy onto the alley head. *Please do not fall into the gutter.* She toweled her ball, gripped her rosin bag, and then stepped to the far left, focusing her sight on the arrows.

One, two, three steps forward, and she released with a snap from her right hand, following through with her arm in the air. Her ball flew down the lane and curved to the right, taking out eight pins. *Shoot!*

"Well, hot damn! You throw a backup ball!"

Candy spun around. "Yes, sir. Took me a few years to figure it out." She gathered her ball up in her towel. "I'm a bit out of practice, though."

Back when she was with her husband, she'd bowled there on a league. Their teammate had helped her figure out her style and throw.

It was plenty fun at first until Jared started acting a fool— getting drunk and starting fights with other bowlers. She'd quit the team and hadn't bowled much since.

"Well, g'on then, pick up your spare." Sterling's deep voice shook her from her thoughts.

She beamed at him over her shoulder and then, turning away, lined up and nailed the spare.

Candy let out a hoot of her own and strolled back toward him, putting a sway in her hips. "You're up, pro."

"All right then." He stood and brushed his hand over her lower back as he passed her.

She shivered at the feel of his calloused palm on her bare skin, sat down, and crossed her legs.

The throbbing in her sex doubled from the contact. *Dear Lord.* One little touch and she was ready to throw him down on the lane and have her way with him.

It scared her a little, the way her body responded to him. Should she be doing this?

Candy drew in a deep breath, trying to calm her body, even just a little. Some regular conversation might help.

Sterling threw his ball, and when he walked back to the return and grabbed his towel, she asked, "So, how'd you hurt your shoulder?"

"Wouldn't believe me if I told ya." He scooped up his ball and proceeded to pick up the spare.

"Wha…" She narrowed her eyes as she watched the pins fall. "You can't be serious?"

Sterling walked back toward her, a staid look on his face. He grabbed his hat, put it on, and tugged it low over his brow. "Serious as a heart attack, ma'am."

"Come on. Tell me." She nudged his hip with her hand.

"You'll laugh."

"I swear I won't." She straightened in her seat.

Good grief, the look on his face was as grim as a voice from the grave. Considering the man had lost his pro status due to the injury, she guessed it was likely a sore subject for him.

"Promise?" He raised his brows.

"Cross my heart." She traced an X on her chest and watched his focus dart to her finger and follow its motion, then back up to meet her gaze.

He cleared his throat and leaned forward in front of her, bracing his hands on his knees.

"All right, listen close, 'cause I'm only gonna say this once."

Candy leaned forward and took a deep breath, preparing herself for whatever the story was.

His warmth and clean, masculine scent washed over her, distracting her for a moment, and she sighed.

They were inches apart, almost nose to nose.

He narrowed his eyes and paused for what felt like forever. Finally, he spoke. "There was a country bar in Tucson. Too much beer. A bet…and a mechanical bull."

He nodded once, never breaking eye contact as if there was nothing more to say on the subject.

Had she heard him right? Candy ran his words through her mind again. Too much beer and what? Confused, she frowned and tilted her head to the side.

Sterling's face softened, and he winked at her.

Oh, Lord, he was kidding. Thank God he was kidding. Candy blew out a nervous breath.

The humor of his words struck home, and she clamped her mouth closed, trying for all it was worth to squash the laugh about to bubble up and burst out of her.

Don't laugh. Do. Not. Laugh. Crap. Oh, my God.

Aaand…she lost the battle.

Candy leaned back in her seat and burst into a fit of giggles so fierce her eyes teared up. Through blurred vision, she watched him straighten and slap his hand over his heart.

"You promised!" he said. "You've broken my heart."

"I'm…sorry." She took a breath. "You're…killin' me…"
Another gasp for air, then more laughter.

Sterling lost his composure and started laughing with her. "Damn! You're cute as hell gigglin' like that."

Candy fanned her face with her hands to cool down a little. "Lordy, I needed that."

"Happy to be your personal comic relief." He sat beside her, a bright smile adorning his sculpted face.

"You still didn't answer my question."

"Sure I did."

"You were drunk and lost a bet with a mechanical bull?"

"Pretty much." He shrugged.

Candy's stomach fell, and she clamped her hand over her mouth and groaned. *Land sakes, he was being serious?*

How could she be so stupid? Now, she felt bad.

The man opened up to her and shared this major thing in his life, and she just laughed in his face. "Oh, my gosh, I'm so sorry. I…I couldn't help it. I thought you were pullin' my leg. I feel like a horse's ass now."

"No need for all that. But no, ma'am, I wasn't pullin' your leg. In truth, I tell it that way 'cause it's too damn embarrassin' to begin with. Better to make a joke about it than have people know what a young fool I was." He plucked up a piece of her hair and ran his fingers down its length. "I like that you laughed. Like I said, you're damn cute when you do."

"I can understand that, but I still feel bad. I'd love to hear the whole story sometime. And I promise, I won't laugh for sure." Candy knew there was more to it than he was letting on.

She felt so bad for laughing and wanted to make it up to him, yes, but God as her witness, she wanted him to tell her the whole story.

"It's not somethin' I share all that often, so you'll have to earn it."

"Earn it, huh? We'll see about that." She paused as an idea struck her. "I think I need a beer." She stood and ran off to grab one.

Maybe she'd have a quick shot while she was behind the bar. A little liquid courage went a long way.

The idea that had sprouted in Candy's mind was wilder than a green-broke stallion. She planned to earn that story out of him, even though he'd be long gone before morning, and she'd likely never get to hear it.

She was more turned on by him than she'd ever been by anyone else, and she couldn't figure out why. Was it his charming, good looks, the mystery around him, or the fact that he made her laugh?

Maybe it was all of the above. There was more to Sterling than met the eye. That, she was sure of.

It didn't matter, though, because she was just going to have a good time with him. It was her chance to be wild and throw all her insecurities out the window.

With a couple ounces of Wild Turkey burning in her belly, she walked back, her beer bottle and another coke for him in hand.

"That was fast." He adjusted his wrist brace.

"I'm good like that." She bumped his hip with hers, then took her turn.

Then, it was Sterling's turn. He bowled his frame and landed another strike.

Candy called on that liquid courage she'd swallowed and went for it. *Here goes nothin'.* "Ever play strip bowling?"

Chapter Five

STERLING LOWERED his head and raised his brows. "You're shittin' me, right?" *Holy hell! Did this sexy slice of heaven seriously just ask me that?*

"You scared, big guy?"

"Mighty bold invitation, if ya ask me." Excitement raced through Sterling like a lightning strike. "What'd ya have in mind, honey?"

"Well, you'll give me a handicap, of course." She pursed her seductive lips.

"I'm thinkin' you're trying to shark me." Sterling laughed. "But I'm also thinkin' this may be one'a those win-win situations I always hear about... So go ahead, what ya got cookin'?"

"Okay, here's the deal. We play reverse score. Lowest pins wins, and you spot me two on every frame." Her eyes showed sheer determination and competition, with just a hint of genuine playfulness. "Anyone caught sandbaggin', the other wins the frame. Deal?"

"Your clothes are gonna look only half as good piled on the floor—" He took a quick sip of his coke. "—As I imagine you will look without them."

"Then it's a deal." She reset the score computer. "You're up first, cowboy... Or should I say stud?"

"Mm-hmm, stud, is it? Feisty filly." He took a step toward the ball return. "I think I'm gonna enjoy this either way."

He hoped he wasn't going to regret it. Rational thought was to focus on the tournament. No distractions, right?

What if this woman turned out to be crazy as hell? What if she became a clinger? Dealing with something along those lines for the next thirty days didn't exactly align with his plan.

"I'm plannin' on it." She took another sip of her beer.

That stopped him short.

With the overwhelming thought of Candy next to him, naked as a jaybird, the pins looked a heck of a lot smaller than he remembered.

And his questions of whether this was a good idea or not were dwindling fast.

He settled into his routine the best he could and managed to knock down seven pins, but still picked up the spare.

Candy took her turn and dropped eight pins, grabbing one more on her second throw. Add two, and she sat at eleven to his ten.

"The shorts, hon." Sterling unwrapped another sucker and popped it in his mouth.

Excitement raced through him, knowing he'd get to see her naked ass. *Thank the Lord for handicaps.*

"You are entirely too satisfied." Her cheeks flushed as she unbuttoned the small denim shorts she was sporting.

Sterling pulled the lollipop from his mouth. "Your rules, if memory serves." He licked his lips. "And I think you may be right—I'm in need of better candy."

She shoved the shorts down and let them drop to her ankles, revealing a tiny red triangle of fabric accentuating her full hips, and kicked them off to one side.

Sterling got slapped with a handicap all his own as his dick thickened behind his fly. There was no way in hell he would maintain any kind of focus in *this* game.

She put her hands on her hips, her fingers framing her tight, narrow stomach, and shifted her weight to one foot. "I'm gonna take your silence to mean I just made your *day*, Mr. Day. I believe it's your turn again."

Sterling chuckled at her cute pun. Damn straight, she'd made his day.

Candy walked over to the half wall and reached for her beer. "Remember, no sandbaggin', or I win the frame."

"Sandbaggin'? No, ma'am. Never." He ran his hand over his short hair and swallowed hard as he eyed her round back-side, displaying a barely there strip of cloth. "Besides, wouldn't be much fun if only one of us was losing their clothes." He smirked and then bowled his frame.

The image of her curvaceous little body, narrow waist flowing into a perfect full ass, and that red thong refused to leave his vision as he willed himself to focus on the arrows laid out before him.

His dick throbbed with the prospect of her choice of clothes on the outcome of this frame.

Pulling on a reserve of focus he didn't realize he had, he unleashed a blur of power and shattered the pin array ahead of him. STRIKE!

As long as she didn't pick up a spare this time, he was losing fabric, and the notion didn't disappoint him in the slightest.

Just as Candy sat in the smooth plastic chair, Sterling threw a strike. *Hot damn!*

She shifted in her seat and crossed her legs, bouncing one

foot as Buckcherry's "Crazy Bitch" started playing through the house speakers.

Sterling turned around with a smug look on his face. "Your turn, sweetness."

He moved to the half wall and took a swallow of his drink.

"View nicer from back there?" She stood, moved to the return, and scooped up her ball.

Realizing he'd now be staring at her bare backside, a swarm of bumblebees buzzed inside her stomach. *Oh Lord, I can't do this.*

Her ass had gotten pretty plump in the few years since Jared had left, but she hadn't much cared until just this moment.

"I'm better able to see your…ah…form from back here." He popped his sucker back in his mouth.

"I bet." She rolled her eyes and stepped onto the lane. *Guess I'm doin' it anyway.*

"Dayum fine form."

She looked over her shoulder to see him standing a handful of feet behind her now, a ravenous look in his eyes.

Lord save me. I haven't wanted anyone to look at me like this in a dog's age.

A thrill blasted through her from the top of her dark blonde head down to the tips of her toes. "Are you trying to distract me, cowboy?"

"I do believe you have the bull by its horns." He stepped closer. "Miss Candy, if you don't mind me sayin', that's one *fine* ass you have there."

She arched a brow and looked down at her bottom. "Glad you like it." She couldn't help feeling pleased as she turned back around and bowled.

Lord in heaven, he liked her ass? *Huh, how 'bout that?*

Distracted, her fingers slipped their grip, and she landed six pins: a two and two split stood proudly at the end of the alleyway. "Get ready to lose your shirt. I can never pick this one up." She threw her second ball to take down the impossible combination of pins and, as she figured, landed only one out of the four. "This would be one time I'm givin' thanks to the split gods."

Sterling stood, a confident look on his face, legs apart, sucker in his mouth, and began unbuttoning his shirt.

Please, don't be wearin' an undershirt. She licked her lips and leaned against the ball return machine as she watched the royal blue material part, button by button, revealing a smooth, muscle-toned body.

His chest had a thin layer of hair traveling into a V and running down the inner line of his six-pack. *Sweet Jesus, the man is fine.* Two small flat areolas, each nipple standing at attention, drew her eyes, and she bit her bottom lip. "Yum."

"Glad you like it." He repeated her earlier comment.

Candy gasped. "I didn't intend to say that out loud." Her cheeks went up in flames.

"You're awful pretty when you do that." He reached for her hand, pulled her against him, and wrapped one arm around her waist.

Candy braced her hands on his bare shoulders and looked up at him. "Do what?" she whispered.

"Get all nervous like, and then blush." He traced his fingers over her cheek, then her mouth. "You taste as sweet as I think?"

She licked her lips. "Try me and find out."

"Damn, girl." He smoothed his hand from her lower back down over one butt cheek. "One minute, you're shy and blushin', and the next, you're full of spit and vinegar." Sterling ran his thumb down her bottom lip, tugging, then releasing it. "Don't mind if I do."

He dipped his head, and Candy rose on tiptoe to meet his lips. *This is really happening.* Her bare thighs and tummy rubbed against his denim-covered legs and hips, and she shivered as tingles spread over her body.

There was no stopping this now. It didn't matter if she never saw him again; she didn't care. Candy wanted this little slice of heaven even if she felt a little wrong for doing it. *Jump, girl. Just jump. It'll be worth it.*

The first contact was soft, gentle. His closed mouth pressed to hers sent smooth waves of desire pulsing down her spine.

She moaned and ran one hand up the back of his neck.

His calloused fingers moved over the bared skin of her backside, then cupped it, hitching her tighter against him. A rumbling growl vibrated against her chest from him when he slid his tongue over her lips.

Candy opened for him. His tongue was warm and smooth as it stroked over hers. My God, he tasted sweet. She gripped the back of his neck, dug her nails in a bit, and pressed her lower body against the erection behind his jeans.

Could she climb him? She was sure willing to try.

The sexual tension building between them exploded in a frenzy of lips, tongues, hands, and nails.

Yes, yes, yes! Too fast. Oh God, don't stop! Wait, finish the game. Tastes so good— Thoughts tumbled over one another as Candy got swept away in a current of pure lust and began drowning in his hot kisses.

She ran one hand down his chest to his side, feeling the velvet softness of his skin, and let out a whimper.

Sterling pulled away first, leaving them both gasping for breath.

He looked down at her, and she saw eyes filled with such deep hunger, she couldn't help but want to dive back in for round two.

"Sweetest candy I've ever had," he whispered, tracing her lips with his fingertips.

She bit the end of his finger when he ventured toward her tongue with it.

"Feisty filly." He swatted her bottom.

Candy yelped at the delicious sting of his palm on her butt cheek, then sucked his finger as he slid it from her mouth. "Your turn."

She licked her lips and pulled away from him. Candy had never been spanked before. It shocked her at first, but what shocked her more was that she liked it.

Would he do it again? She sure as heck hoped so.

Chapter Six

STERLING'S HEART thundered in his ears, almost drowning out Garth Brooks's "Friends in Low Places" playing on the overhead speakers.

As he approached the ball return, the image of her perfect ass set in that red thong made a triumphant return to the forefront of his mind. *She picked one hell of a game to get me flustered.*

He drew in a deep breath, letting it out as he grabbed his towel from the edge of the return.

"What's the matter, stud? Balls got you spooked?" she teased from behind him.

"Don't you worry about me—" He looked over his shoulder against his better judgment to find her running her tongue over the lollipop she'd taken from him earlier and staring at his backside. "You tryin' to kill me here? Good Lord, woman!"

Less distractions? My ass. Sterling knew his manager hadn't seen this coming. This stay was supposed to be all business. No pleasure.

"Is it working?"

Hell yeah, it's workin'. He fought hard not to reply. Tried even harder not to scoop her off her feet and plant another kiss on those luscious lips.

Sterling shook his head, inhaled deep, and exhaled through his nose, reaching for some measure of calm. *Okay, not helping.*

Turning back, he picked up his ball and rolled it in the towel in his hand. His eyes drifted to the arrows on the waxed lane, and he stifled the urge to take one more glance over his shoulder.

Stepping to his mark, he set his jaw, allowed his vision to narrow, and proceeded to bowl. The heavy crunch of the pins was music to his ears, but he found himself at odds with the outcome.

Six pins fell. In a typical game, that would send his mind racing for the proper target to pick up the spare. This time, he wished he didn't have a second ball to throw.

"You got it in you to pick this one up?" Candy chimed in. Her teasing tone forced a hitch in his breathing.

"Ahem… You gonna let me bowl? Or you worried about catching a draft in here?" He teased back.

He let the ball fly, and it hugged the gutter for an instant too long. It cranked hard to the left and knocked down the two back pins. *Dammit. Wait! Yee-haw!*

He'd never found himself so at war with his intentions. His whole life and career had relied on his ability to outscore his opponents consistently. To edge them out when it counted.

Now, he was playing to lose so that he could win. Could it get any more contradicting?

"Shit." He turned to head back to his seat. "I let it hang too long."

"Guess I do have you spooked," she mocked him, beaming the whole time. "Now who's worried about catching a draft?"

"Did you forget your rules already?" he countered, spanking her bare ass as she walked by him. "Reverse scores, remember? And no sandbaggin'."

She rubbed her bottom. "Then I guess you better hope I do better than six pins."

"Oh, I'm hoping all right."

Sterling had to adjust his throbbing erection as she bent forward with her ball to focus. She was taunting him with that luscious ass of hers. He was sure of it. Damn if it didn't do the trick.

Her hips swayed like a pendulum on a grandfather clock as she made her approach. The resounding crack following the release of her ball shook him out of the trance he found himself in. Strike!

Guess she ain't sandbaggin'.

"Praise the heavens, 'bout time!"

"Damn, girl, feel good, don't it?" He loved watching her flush with excitement.

"Heck yeah, it does." She beamed back at him. "You must love the feeling."

"Why do you think I play so hard?"

That feeling was exactly what drove Sterling to win at all costs. It filled him up and set him on fire, even to the point of throwing his career away to win a drunken bet on a mechanical bull. Bottom line was, Sterling won the bet but lost his career.

"You're up, big guy." She started for the half wall.

"Ahem..."

"Huh?"

"I believe you're forgettin' somethin', hon, must be all the excitement." Sterling couldn't have used a crowbar to pry his eyes off her. "Time to say goodbye to that sexy little shirt of yours."

"Oh dear." She turned toward him. "I think you may be right. Where *are* my manners?"

She locked her beautiful green eyes with his and let her fingers drift over her breasts as they found their way to the knot in the front of her shirt.

Speechless, he leaned forward in his seat in anticipation as she pulled the fabric out of its controlled tangle and then released the two buttons she had clasped.

Sterling was sure he was going to pass out from blood loss —every drop rocketing toward his already throbbing shaft. *Tournament? What tournament?*

A flash of clarity penetrated his lust-induced haze. The last time Sterling had done something so wild, he'd lost his spo — *Oh, got-dayum!*

Sterling's battle in his mind was lost as she opened her shirt, revealing a red lace bra, leaving little to the imagination. Pert nipples struggled hard behind the sheer pattern to press their way out as she held her arms behind her to let her shirt fall off her shoulders and slip down her arms.

Catching it with one hand, she made a sexy display of holding her shirt out and releasing it to join her shorts on the floor.

"Sweet Jesus." He ran his hand over his mouth to keep himself from drooling.

"Now, I believe it's your move." She paused and bit her lower lip. "I mean, turn."

CANDY STOOD THERE, almost naked at this point in the game, with no shame or embarrassment. It was amazingly freeing, baring herself to him in this way. By the look on his face, he liked what he saw, too.

Her nipples throbbed behind the lace fabric of her bra, aching for the touch of his hands and mouth, and the moisture from her sex coated her silk thong.

She leaned against the back counter and crossed her legs

at the ankle, squeezing her thighs together, trying to find a little relief from the steady pulsing in her clit.

At this rate, they would run out of clothes before they finished all ten frames. That suited her just fine because she was ready to jump his bones here and now.

Thank God there weren't any security cameras she needed to worry about. This night of naughtiness would be her little secret and was right up her alley…all puns and pins intended.

"Woman, you have me so hard for you right now, I can barely stand it." He adjusted the obvious erection in his jeans.

He smoothed his big palm down over the bulge, and she about lost her mind.

"I hope, for the love of God, you have some condoms," she said, her voice gone raspy and deep.

She cupped both breasts in her hands and tweaked her nipples through the thin fabric.

"I got 'em. Thankfully, because I don't usually." He gripped himself through the denim and then licked his lips. "Do that again."

"What?" Candy looked down at her breasts. "This?" She squeezed her cleavage together, pinching her nipples again. Closing her eyes, she let out a moan. "Fuck, it feels good."

"You keep tempting me with those gorgeous tits and talkin' all dirty like, and this game's gonna be over right quick."

"I can't help it. You got me all in a lather and ready to go. Bowl your turn before I lose it, cowboy."

"I plan on slippin' and slidin' in all your lather. You can bet your sweet, fine ass on it."

Line drawn in the sand, he turned, grabbed his ball and lined up his shot.

She snagged her beer and took a long swig as she watched the muscles in his back flex when he threw his ball. Good God, she wanted him.

He landed eight out of the ten pins and then picked up

Dorothy F. Shaw & T. D. Hoffman

the spare, which meant if she was going to see his pants come off, she needed to bowl a lower count.

Not a problem. She shook so badly with thoughts of his hands on her body again and more of those drugging kisses, she'd lost her ability to concentrate.

Candy trailed her fingertips over his chest as she walked to the lane. When she scooped up her ball, his hands came to rest on her hips from behind, and she straightened against him.

"Mr. Day, are you tryin' to distract me?" She gasped when he moved his hands around to her stomach and then ran them up her body to cup her heavy breasts.

"Not intentionally, Miss Jameson. I just can't seem to deny myself this one touch." He ran his mouth over her shoulder and squeezed her breasts together. "They fit my hands perfectly."

Her breath hitched, and she arched her back, pressing her round ass against his stiff prick. "You do have really big… hands," she said on an exhale.

He nipped her shoulder and released her. "Your move."

Dang, she couldn't focus at all now. Her breasts were a D cup, and his hands fit them as if they'd been made just for her.

Candy's heart pounded as her pulse raced out of control, her body gone boneless and hot with need.

She stepped up and threw her ball, taking out three pins. Candy dropped her head forward and shook it.

He snorted.

Taking her second ball, she downed another three. With the handicap, she totaled eight. Meaning: His pants were coming off.

Sweet Jesus, it was all she could do not to jump for joy. Hands on her hips, she turned and faced him.

He was leaning against the back wall, arms crossed over his chest, looking so hungry it made her suck in her breath.

40

Her channel clenched with need for him, and more wetness coated her panties.

"Pants," she demanded.

"C'mere and take 'em off for me."

"If I take those jeans off you, we won't be finishin' this game."

"As much as I want to see you throw your ball with no bra on, I'm fine with you down on your knees in front of me."

She gasped, and her stomach clenched. Visions of sucking him deep into her mouth played before her eyes, and her feet began to move, carrying her over to him with no hesitation at all.

He removed his wrist brace and set it down, and as she knelt before him, he straightened from his lean on the wall. "So we callin' it a tie?"

"Agreed." She grabbed his belt buckle, loosened it, and tugged it open. Next came his fly. Pop, pop, pop went each button. Staring up at him, she guided his pants over his hips but left his boxers in place.

Leaning in, she licked the soft, thin line of hair running down his six-pack. His skin's clean, salty flavor burst over her tongue, and his scent flooded her senses, causing her to hum in appreciation. *Oh yeah, baby.*

His stomach muscles tightened beneath her touch.

Sterling groaned, then buried one hand in her thick hair. "Wicked thing."

Chapter Seven

Sterling's mind raced, and bowling became the *last* thing in the mix.

Everything about this woman had him tingling from head to toe and just kept getting better.

The moan he received when he gripped her hair told him she was feeling the same way.

Candy ran her fingers up his exposed thighs, digging them in just enough to show she was the one in control at the moment.

She nipped at his skin just above his waistband and slipped her fingers between the elastic and his abdomen.

Tugging the boxers down his hips, she stopped when his cock made it hard to pass without extra attention.

He grunted as the waistband caught at his erection. Letting go of her hair, he went to slide off his boxers. "Need a hand?"

She slapped his hand away and shook her head. "No way. This is all mine."

She licked her lips and tucked her hand inside his boxers. Wrapping her fingers around his length, she yanked his pants and boxers to his ankles with the other.

Her eyes sparkled as she looked back up at him and ran her tongue over her bottom lip.

As she licked the shaft from base to tip, his heart pounded, and his breath rushed in and out of his lungs. When she dragged her tongue in a slow circle around the ridge of the head, heat blazed a path through Sterling's veins.

Candy worked her hand up and down in measured strokes before sucking him inside her mouth.

With a groan, he let his head fall back as the warm, wet seal of her lips sent electricity racing over his entire body.

She cupped his heavy sac and sucked him to the back of her throat for several strokes, stopping to tease the underside of his crown with the soft tip of her tongue.

A bead of slick arousal eased from the tip of his dick. Candy darted her pink tongue out, tasting it before drawing him back inside.

Sterling brushed his fingers through her hair as he bent over and trailed his hand down her back to the clasp of her bra. He popped the hook and let the sides flap free. "This needs to come off."

She dug her fingers into his backside, making him grunt out a heavy breath before she sat back and gazed up at him. Her straps drifted off her shoulders as she removed the lace cups from her heaving breasts and tossed the bra to the side.

"Is this better?" Propping her hands on her thighs and arching her back, her arms framed her beautiful tits, pushing them forward.

"Oh Lord, yes. You *are* gorgeous." He toed each bowling shoe off and shed the remainder of his clothing.

Sterling tucked his hands under her arms, drawing her upright and against his body. He found her lips eager and waiting as he teased them with his tongue and then deepened the kiss, leaving her humming in return.

He drew her bottom lip into his mouth and bit down, dragging his teeth across the delicate flesh as he released her from his kiss. "Mmm...I need to taste how sweet my new Candy is."

Lifting her, Sterling urged her legs around his hips and then turned to place her on top of the half wall.

"Don't tease me now." She yelped as her full ass touched the cool laminate top.

"I don't tease." His fingers looped around the thin fabric of her thong at her hips and glided it down her thighs.

Her bare pussy glistened in the overhead lights, and Sterling licked his lips in hunger.

God, she's beautiful, head to toe.

He pressed his large hands against her thighs and widened her legs farther. Leaning forward, he trailed a line up the inside of one thigh with his tongue and nipped at her skin next to her slick folds.

"Lord have mercy." Candy smoothed her hands over the top of his head, down the back of his neck to the juncture at his shoulders. Digging her nails in, she pulled him closer and let out a deep, guttural moan.

CANDY WAS ready to jump out of her skin. A scream hovered just at the tip of her tongue; she needed to feel his mouth on her pussy now! *Just a little...closer!*

Sterling smirked as she tugged on the back of his neck. "Patience, darlin'." He blew a soft breath over her slit.

"I've never been a big fan of—"

He flicked his tongue over her clit.

"Oh God! Fan of—"

Another lick.

"Fan of what, sugar?" He leaned in and sucked the tight

bundle of nerves between his lips, pressing his tongue against it.

"Fuck. Oh, yes, like that." She let go of his head to grip the edge of the half wall.

"Mmm. Sweeter than honey," he mumbled against her wet flesh.

She jerked against his face when he latched on to her clit again, sucking and flicking his tongue against it. He went to work on her like a man having his last meal.

As he licked and nibbled at her outer lips, she raised her legs over his shoulders and held on for dear life.

When Sterling entered her with two long fingers, her head fell back, and she let out the scream that'd been lying in wait for the last ten minutes.

He paused and looked up at her with his gorgeous blue eyes. "I'm gonna make you come so hard for me, you'll forget both our names."

He returned to his mission, settling into a rhythm that matched the rocking of her hips with the thrust of his fingers while keeping his mouth locked in place around her clit.

Candy's orgasm began to wake and stretch like a lazy cat deep inside her belly, climbing from its hiding place to make itself known. Spotting its prey, it ran forward, slamming into her, taking her over the edge with the force of a Texas summer storm and rocking her body harder than any earthquake on the planet.

She screamed again, long and loud, as her climax rumbled through her.

Sterling slid his hands beneath her ass, scooped her up from the wall, and carried her to the wood floor of the bowling lane. He laid her down and covered her body with his.

"Condom." She gasped for breath as she writhed against him.

"Damn." He rose from her and ran back to his pants,

returning a moment later with the small foil package between his fingers, his dick standing at full attention.

"Let me." She sat up and gripped his cock in her hand, pumping it in a slow rhythm as he pulled the condom from the foil wrapper.

"Woman, I won't last long if you keep workin' me like this." He handed her the latex ring to put on.

"Mmm." She rolled the condom over the head and then sheathed him to the base. "Tight fit on this nice thick prick of yours." She cupped his sac, massaging it. "What if you don't fit?" She batted her lashes, pretending innocence.

"Sweetheart, you're nice and wet, and you're gonna enjoy every bit of muscle-strainin' work I'll need to do to make it fit."

"Oh, my Lord." She bit her lip and lay back down. She couldn't wait to feel him fill her. Couldn't wait to feel the delicious stretch of her cunt as he sank deep inside.

Sterling kneeled between her spread thighs and placed the tip of his length at her entrance.

Candy ran her hands over her breasts, cupped and squeezed them, then pinched her nipples. "Come on, cowboy. Let's see what ya got."

He slid just the head in. "Careful." He blew out a breath. "That smart mouth of yours is bound to land you on your hands and knees with this spankable ass of yours high in the air." He pressed in a little deeper and groaned.

She watched wide-eyed as he closed his mouth, and a muscle ticked in his jaw.

Holy sweet mother of God and all the saints. Her body trembled as he moved farther inside her channel, inch by incredible inch, stretching her. "So good. Cowboy, you feel so good." She reached for his arms and gripped them hard, digging her nails in.

He growled and pulled back out, then glided into her, this time faster and with enough force to make her breasts sway on her chest. "Hell, woman, the sight of those gorgeous tits of yours jiggling for me is damn near about to send me over the edge."

"So be it. I'll be game for round two." She let go of his arms to lick a fingertip on each hand and run them around the edges of her areolas. "Or three."

He grunted, pulled out again, and drilled into her with a slap, sending her scooting backward toward the pins.

"Yes! Harder!" She raised her knees.

He gripped her legs, cursed, and slammed into her again, and once again, she slid backward toward the foul line.

"You plannin' on sending me down the lane? Fresh grease and all, it—"

Another hard slam pulled a high-pitched cry from her lungs.

"First time for everything." He leaned forward, braced himself on one arm, and sucked a nipple into his mouth.

"Makes two of us." She gritted her teeth and braced for the next thrust. Lordy, this was amazing.

Candy arched against his mouth and wrapped her legs around his waist. *She* had *never* been like this before. The dirty words pouring out of her mouth shocked her and thrilled her at the same time. So raw and erotic. And she wanted more— needed more.

God help her. Even if he stopped now, she'd die a properly fucked young woman.

Chapter Eight

ONE... Thrust. *More*... Thrust. *Little*... Sterling gripped her hips as he drove hard inside her tight channel. *Shove*... Buzz!

The red foul line indicators lit up as the warning buzzer sounded, signifying he'd reached his goal. Shifting his weight up off his hands until he was upright again, he thrust one more time, sending Candy farther down the waxed boards.

"Sterling!"

He grabbed her by the ankle and tugged her back to him. "Where do you think you're gettin' off to?" His rock-hard cock bounced in time with his abrupt movements. "I'm not done with you yet."

Candy squealed as her ass slipped along the maple, returning to him. "I should hope not. If you're nice, I won't count the foul line...this time."

He gripped her thighs, pulling her close until her ass bumped tight against his heavy sac, and laid a shapely leg over each of his own. "And if I'm not nice?" He raised one brow.

"Then you may earn extra points," she challenged.

Sterling grabbed both ankles and raised her legs toward the ceiling. Shifting them to one hand, he pulled her up, lifting her ass off the floor.

"Now, what do you have in—"

SLAP!

Her ass reddened from the impact of his large hand, launching an echo around the wide space and bouncing off the brown-paneled walls despite the loud music.

She whimpered, and a brief look of shock washed across her face as she rubbed her flushed ass cheek, but then a playful gleam in her eyes and a devilish grin took its place.

"On your hands and knees, darlin'." Releasing her ankles, he flipped her over and guided her backward toward him until her fingers were just shy of the foul line. He gripped her hips tight as he lined up behind her. Teasing her slick cunt with his swollen crown, he plunged deep inside her.

Candy let her head fall forward as she whimpered, her lush locks splaying out in front of her on the slim maple boards.

He pulled out slowly, making sure she felt every inch of him, before slamming back inside her.

"There will be a penalty every time the little red foul light goes off," he said in a low rumble as he thrust harder.

Her moans grew louder in time with his increasing thrusts.

He kept his hands rooted on her hips, and he couldn't remove his eyes from the beauty of her full, heart-shaped ass.

As if testing his warning, she inched one hand forward to cross the foul line. Her reward? Another sting to her backside. "Oh God!" she bit out.

"Go ahead, do it again." His words fought past his groans. "I love the way your ass looks when it's all red." He rubbed his hand over her warm butt cheek and continued to fuck her harder and faster, taunting her.

She pressed against him with her backside, an encouragement, he assumed, to thrust harder.

Their sweaty bodies smacked together in a fanatical, hunger-driven rhythm.

Candy scooted her other hand across the foul line.

He could feel her pussy spasm tight around his dick when his hand found its target on her ass cheek again.

Sex had never been anything like this, and it sent a tangled web of thoughts traveling through his mind. Her raw energy, her passion and how responsive she was to each touch overwhelmed him, causing his release to build.

He wanted every bit of her she gave him and more.

"Harder, cowboy," she ground out past her heavy breathing. "Fuck me harder. I'm gonna come."

He slapped her ass one last time and pulled her hips tight to his pelvis. "Followin' you over."

"Oh my God!" She reached between her legs and began rubbing her clit.

He had a death grip on her hips as he slammed into her, his scrotum tightening between his legs as his orgasm tingled at the base of his spine.

Her pussy clamped around his thick shaft, squeezing his length, as her climax ran through her.

He held her tight to his groin as his orgasm hit, forcing the breath from his chest, and he growled out her name while his semen boiled up and pulsed from his cock. Breathless, Sterling collapsed over her luscious body.

"Oh, my Lord. That was amazing." She panted, her back heaving under him.

"You ain't kiddin', sweetheart." He ran his hand around her waist and then pulled them both over to lie on their sides together. He curled around her, throwing one leg over hers, as they both let their breathing calm.

"Can't say this was in the plan when I woke up this morning." Candy ran her hand over his thigh.

He nipped her shoulder. "Not in my wildest dreams, sugar." Forget dreams. She'd come straight out of his fantasies, and all he could think about was how long he'd have to wait to get a taste of her sweetness again.

Strawn, Texas, *definitely* had the best candy around for miles—with a capital C.

CANDY LET OUT a little purr as she wiggled closer within the nest of Sterling's body. But as her own body began to cool, coming down from the high of her orgasm, her mind raced.

Had they really just had sex? In the bowling alley? On the frickin' lane? *Ohh. Myy. God! What did I just do?*

Sterling shifted behind her, and she took it as her cue to get up.

"Hey, you okay?"

"Yeah, I'm fine." She turned and headed in search of her clothes…which were scattered everywhere…for Lord's sake, she still had her bowling shoes on. Locating her panties, she pulled them on and then found her bra.

He rose from his spot on the floor and watched her. "That's woman-speak for 'not fine.'"

Not sure what to say, she decided on nothing and ignored his comment. She'd never done something so foolhardy and wild. In a matter of hours, she'd gone against everything she'd been avoiding for what seemed like forever. If anyone found out about this, she'd never live it down.

An uncomfortable silence fell between them as he gathered his clothes, and she finished putting hers on.

"I'll be right back." He kissed her cheek and headed toward the men's room, his clothes bundled in his hands.

She watched him walk away, admiring his perfect ass even with her sudden grim mood. *Crap.* Candy slipped on her shorts and fastened her little top in place.

She didn't do one-night stands; it wasn't her thing. And

didn't that just suck? *Probably shoulda' thought of that before you went all nekkid and buck wild.*

This wasn't who she was. Candy Jameson was a nice girl. She didn't sleep around or have sex with strange men!

Sterling returned after a bit...fully clothed. "Damn, it's late. I better get goin'." He smothered a yawn behind his hand.

"Me, too. Well, it was real nice meetin' you." Feeling awkward, she held her hand out to shake his.

"Don't hurt my feelings, darlin'." He grabbed her hand and pulled her against his chest. "Don't I get a goodnight kiss?"

"Oh, I just..." She circled his neck with her arms. "I guess I'm not very good at this."

Sterling bent and brushed his mouth over hers. "So sweet," he whispered, then kissed her again.

Candy shivered from the tender contact and opened for him. Her body melted against his as he caressed her lips and tongue.

He pulled away and gazed down at her, his pretty blue eyes sparkling. "May I walk you to your car?"

"With a kiss like that, how could I say no?" She patted his chest. "Get your stuff."

"Yes, ma'am." He did as she asked.

Candy grabbed her purse from behind the counter and shut down the remaining lights in the alley.

He stepped outside and waited for her as she set the alarm unit, exited and then locked the building.

"I'm parked just over there." She pointed.

"Lead the way." He rested his hand on the small of her back as they started walking toward her car.

She shivered again but rubbed her arms as though the chill in the night air bothered her.

Truth was, it was the feel of his calloused hand on her

lower back that made her skin prickle into goosebumps. She liked it. A lot.

"Bit of a chill in the air," he said.

"The nights have been gettin' cooler for sure." She dug in her purse for her keys. "Well, here I am." She unlocked her car door and opened it.

"I had a real nice time, Candy."

"Me, too." She tossed her purse onto the front seat.

Sterling turned her toward him and then circled her waist with his arms.

She met his gaze and let him kiss her one last time.

"Take care of yourself." She let her hands fall to his shoulders. "And good luck in that tournament."

"Thanks. I'll be seein' ya, Candy." He placed a gentle kiss on her cheek.

She pulled from his embrace and settled in the front seat of her car. "Yeah, sure."

Sterling smiled. "You'll see." He closed the door for her.

Candy backed out of the space and pulled away, giving him a wave as she passed him.

"Be seeing me? Probably not, cowboy. But it's a nice thought," she mumbled as she glanced at him in the rearview mirror.

What the heck had he meant by that, anyway? She wouldn't be seeing him again. He'd be gone by morning, and God willing, she'd escape anyone finding out about her little slip. *I won't be* seeing *anythin'.* It was how it *had* to be.

Chapter Nine

THE NEXT DAY, after unpacking and settling into his room, Sterling headed for breakfast at Flossie's. It was a short walk down Main Street.

Hell, everything was a short walk in this small town.

When he was done eating, he strolled down the sidewalk to see just where he'd landed. Every one of the buildings and businesses occupying them looked as if time had stopped in the mid-fifties.

Circling back, he ended up at the bowling alley in search of Mason.

Sterling stepped up to the front desk. "Howdy, I'm looking for Mason Jennings."

"You don't look like a bill collector."

"No, sir, can't say I am. My manager sent me here and said to ask for Mason."

"Ah. Then you must be Sterling Day." He stuck his hand out to shake. "You found me. I'm Mason, and this here is Bowling Dreams."

"Nice to meet ya." Sterling grasped the man's hand and greeted him properly.

"Troy said you were gearing up for a bit of a comeback in

Fort Worth next month. How ya feelin' about that?" Mason leaned his elbows on the counter.

"Pretty good. Actually, pretty damn good." Sterling fished a sucker out of his shirt pocket and unwrapped it.

"Like hearin' that." Mason rubbed the back of his neck. "Tried my luck at the pro circuit myself. Turned out Dad's shoes were a bit too big to fill. Guess I'm better behind the counter than on the lanes."

"Well, as long as I keep this shoulder in check, I think I'm throwin' better than I ever have." Sterling popped the sucker in his mouth.

"Troy filled me in on your plan, and he believes in ya, so he pulled in a few favors, and here we are. You can have run of the lanes as much as you need till you head out. Food and alcohol, you have to cover, but cokes are on the house. You win? You mention us in any interview you can squeeze us into. Deal?"

"Can't argue with that, and I appreciate it, Mason." Sterling stuck his hand out to seal the deal. "I don't plan on losin' neither." He could not imagine himself happy being stuck in a small town running an alley instead of competing in one.

"I'm here most days, and I'll introduce you to my night manager. I'll fill the staff in on you, and you just do your thing... That'd be winning."

"Fair enough." He liked this guy already. Straight to the point and seemed genuinely interested in Sterling making his way back to the pros. Now, it was up to Sterling to make it happen.

"How 'bout I put you down on lane three? Nobody should bother you there." Mason looked at his computer screen.

"If it's not too much trouble, I'm kinda partial to ten. Right out in the middle of everything."

"Fine by me if you don't think you'll be bothered."

"Not like it can be any worse than playing a tournament. Besides, ten recently became my lucky number." Sterling reached for his bag and wondered if Mason regretted not making it to the pros or if he was honestly content where he ended up.

"All yours." Mason gestured toward the lane directly across from the counter. "Have at it."

CANDY SLAPPED BLINDLY at her buzzing alarm clock, seeking the snooze button. Good Lord, she was tired.

She'd tossed and turned half the night, her mind filled with thoughts of Sterling and what they'd done in the alley.

She'd never been the type of girl to have a one-night stand, but heck, it'd been forever since she'd had sex.

Even if a little bit of shame threatened to rise at her behavior, it wasn't enough to drown out the butterflies that took flight when she thought of how good every naughty minute of it felt.

And she'd never see him again anyway. No harm done.

Candy turned over and tried for a few more minutes of sleep before her alarm buzzed again. Silencing it, she pulled the sheets back and sat up.

She winced as the slight aches in her body, the product of some long overdue loving, made themselves known. She looked down and noticed her knees were bruised, too.

Good Lord, what did her backside look like? Sterling had spanked her so many times she'd lost count. She giggled at the thought, rose from the bed and headed for the shower.

The hot water eased some of the soreness out of her muscles and woke her up fully. After doing her hair and makeup, she sat down at the table in the little kitchen of her trailer and had breakfast.

According to the time, it was past noon, but it was still morning for her.

After spending the day taking care of her normal Saturday activities, braving the crowds at the Shoppin' Basket to restock her cupboards, and filling the car with gas, she headed back to her trailer and changed for work.

Sterling drifted into her mind on occasion, and she'd sigh, loving that she had a secret that would keep her going for a long while.

Candy arrived at work a little earlier than she needed to. Antsy enough to jump out of her skin, she figured she'd stop in the alley bar and chat with Trudie for a bit, though no way she would be sharing her secret with her.

Trudie was sweet, but she was the gossip queen of town. And Candy didn't want *anyone* knowing her business.

"Howdy, Trudie!" Candy took a seat on one of the black vinyl bar stools.

"Hey there, darlin'. Don't you just look cute as a button tonight?" Trudie leaned across the bar top and gave Candy a peck on the cheek. "What brings you in early?"

"Nothin' much, just feelin' a little antsy. How's your day goin' so far?"

Trudie placed a glass of Diet in front of her. "My day got a whole lot more interestin' when I saw tall, cool and delicious was back and bowling on lane ten again."

Candy started choking on the drink of coke she'd barely swallowed. "What'd you say?" she squeaked out as she reached for a napkin and coughed a few more times.

"My Lord, child. Are you okay?"

Candy wiped her mouth. "What'd you say?"

"The good pickin's that was in last night is here. Mason said he's gonna be in town for the next month, training for that tourney in Fort Worth." Trudie turned to set some new bottles on the back ledge. "Guess he'll be in most days, maybe nights, too."

"You sure it's the same guy?"

"Sugar, I never make a mistake where a good-lookin' man is concerned. You know better than that." Trudie jerked her chin toward the exit into the alley. "Go see for yourself."

"All right then." Candy rose from her seat and headed for the doors.

Shit fire and save the matches. Sterling was going to be here for a month? No, Trudie had to be mistaken. Good Lord, she hoped the woman was mistaken. Candy couldn't see him again. That's not how this was supposed to work.

She peeked her head out, and clear as day, on that darn lane ten, stood tall, cool and delicious, lining up a shot.

Holy crap. What the heck am I gonna do now?

Chapter Ten

STRIKE!

The pins shattered in the tenth frame, and Sterling watched every one of them fall as if he'd walked down the lane and kicked them over himself.

Damn, he was feeling good and wanted that championship so bad he could taste it. His ball traveled back up the return and came to rest as Sterling stared at his score array on the overhead monitor.

All strikes except three frames, in which he still managed to pick up the spares. *Come on, ol' man, you got one more in ya.*

With an arsenal of determination stored up, Sterling picked up his ball and went through his tried-and-true routine as he stepped to the line and unleashed a blur of spinning blue and silver down the boards.

Again, he held his form and watched the pins fall.

All of them.

The crash echoed off the lanes. Ever since he started bowling, that resounding explosion of pins always painted a picture of splinters flying everywhere. He knew it was a ridiculous thought, but it made him laugh every time.

Time to ice the shoulder, do some stretching and grab

dinner, not necessarily in that order. Sitting down, he unlaced and removed his bowling shoes, replacing them with his slightly worn cowboy boots.

As he packed away his wrist brace in his bag, something, or rather, someone, caught his attention out of the corner of his eye.

Sure enough, there was Candy. Trying her best not to be obvious and failing.

This was going to be one interesting month if she was planning on hiding in the shadows the whole time. Sterling had found it hard enough to shake off the constant flashbacks of the night before so he could practice.

The thought of her bouncing around the alley just out of arm's reach was enough to send his heart racing in frustration. One thing was for sure: he was not done with that girl. Not in the slightest.

His manager's voice echoed through his mind, reminding him to focus and avoid distractions.

Yet even with the replays of his first encounter with Candy threatening to take his mind off the game, he seemed to be dead on almost every time he sent the ball down the lane.

Maybe there was such a thing as a good distraction.

She was gone by the time he'd finished packing his ball away. Determined to find her, Sterling hefted the bag off the ground and headed for the bar.

He found the second entrance to the bar farther down the alley from where he first spied her looking out. Maybe he could outflank her and surprise her.

Sterling walked into the dimly lit lounge and found his target half sitting on a stool and leaning up with her elbows on the bar top, talking to the woman slinging drinks.

She was still as beautiful as he remembered, and it was hard to pull his eyes away from her sexy curves and, damn, all that thick dirty blonde hair cascading over her shoulders.

He walked up behind her and let his bag drop to the floor

beside her stool. The loud thunk made Candy squeak in surprise, and she practically fell off her perch.

Sterling tipped his hat. "Howdy, ma'am. Care to say hello to an ol' cowboy?"

"You really shouldn't sneak up on a girl like that. 'Bout gave me a heart attack." Candy's cheeks flushed bright red. "And what's with the ma'am stuff?"

"Just bein' polite and failing at being cute, I guess." He leaned against the side of the bar. Had she lost interest already?

Looking over at the bartender, he extended his hand to greet her. "Howdy, I'm Sterling Day, nice to meet ya."

"Hey, sugar, I'm Trudie Bennett." She popped her gum. "Get ya anything, hon?"

"Regular coke would be great, thanks. Need a refill?" He looked back to Candy to find she had a look on her face as though she'd seen a white rabbit and had gone down the hole in pursuit of Alice. "You okay, Candy?"

She blinked. "Huh? No, thank you, Trudie's got me covered. Plus, my shift starts in a few minutes, and I'm gonna have to go clock in soon."

"Guess that means I can't invite you to join me for dinner tonight." Sterling swirled his drink with his straw, debating whether that was the best idea considering his agenda for the month.

He had too much riding on his goal to go pro again, but screw it; he was going for it anyway. The sex was amazing, and he genuinely liked Candy.

"Really? Dinner? Ain't you the sweetest thang." Trudie forced her way into the conversation. "Ain't that sweet?" She smacked Candy's elbow.

She rubbed her elbow and glared in Trudie's direction. "Knock it off. You know I can't." She looked back at Sterling. "Thank you, really, but I do have to work tonight."

"Well, I can appreciate that. How 'bout it, though?

Another night?" Sterling sipped his drink. "You can't possibly have to work every night." Hope coursed through his body as his mind raced with how well they'd fit the night before.

"You want me to go check your schedule right quick, hon?" Trudie beamed.

Candy stared back at Trudie and practically growled, "That isn't necessary, thank you. I can check my own schedule."

"Lighten up, sweetie. Ya gotta eat sometime." Trudie crossed her arms over her chest.

"Tell ya what, I'm thinkin' I caught you off guard." He placed a hand on hers. "Go work your shift. Give it some thought. I'll be here all month, and the offer stands."

Sterling turned back to Trudie. "Where do you recommend eatin' around here? I know you gotta have a favorite place."

"Favorite? Well, the Brandin' Iron is probably one of the best sit-downs around here, that or Flossie's. But if you just want to get something to go, the Pak-a-Sak is your best bet." Trudie finished drying off a couple tall glasses and placed them back on their shelf.

"Pak-a-Sak, huh?" Sterling tipped his chin and raised an eyebrow. "Since I won't have company just yet, I think I may just have to check that place out tonight. Much obliged, Trudie." Sterling pulled a five from his wallet and slid it toward Trudie. "Mason said cokes are on the house, but here's a tip for you." He smiled. "You ladies have yourselves a good night. I'll see y'all soon."

Sterling picked up his bowling bag and headed toward the exit, turning his head to look back at Candy one more time.

CANDY WATCHED Sterling exit the bar to the parking lot. She turned back to Trudie and hung her head in her hands. "Oh God. This can't be happenin'."

"What in Sam Hill has gotten into you?"

"I seem to have lost my dang mind, that's what."

"I guess so, seein' as though you just turned down a dinner date with tall, cool and delicious." Trudie leaned forward and crossed her arms in front of her on the bar top. "Dish."

Candy groaned. "Just let it go."

Trudie snorted. "You know by now that ain't gonna happen."

"I need to get clocked in." Candy stood.

"That's fine, but—" Trudie narrowed her gaze. "—You let me know when you're ready to talk about it."

"Thanks. See you later, Trudie."

"Bye, sugar. Remember, I'll be here all night."

Candy left the bar and clocked in for her shift. A month? He was going to be here for a whole month? How the heck could she avoid him?

Sweet Lord, it was just supposed to be a one-night stand! Get a little play between the sheets or, in her case, on the bowling lane and move on down the road.

And now he wanted to take her to dinner?

She walked behind the front counter in a daze, blew past Mason, and put her purse in the back office.

"Hello to you, too," Mason said when she returned with a fresh cash drawer in her hands.

"Hey. Sorry." She placed the drawer on the counter. "You ready to shift over?"

"Sure am." Mason stretched and then pulled his drawer from the register. "Oh, one thing, there's gonna be a guy here from New Mexico for the next few weeks, final training for the tourney in Fort Worth. Name's Sterling Day."

Candy nodded and deposited her drawer in the register.

"His lane time's free." He stepped away from the counter and into the back office.

Thanks for the update. Candy rolled her eyes and grabbed the clipboard for the night's Rock-n-Bowl sign-ups. There weren't many. Crap, maybe they'd get some walk-ins.

"Have a good night, Candy." Mason stepped around the counter.

"You, too. Tell Shirley hey for me." She set the clipboard down.

Time to get herself together. Chances were good Sterling wouldn't be back tonight.

Maybe she'd get lucky, and he'd just be practicing during the day.

She glanced at lane ten, and the images of the night before flashed in her mind, sending a bolt of lust through her tummy and down between her thighs.

The man had some moves, that was for sure. She rubbed her hand over her butt cheek, remembering the sting he'd left there.

Maybe she should let him take her to dinner. She just had to make sure no one in town found out about it.

Thanks to her ex, she'd had more than her fill of small-town gossip living in Strawn, and she sure as heck didn't want to deal with it again.

Chapter Eleven

THE WHOLE VIBE of Bowling Dreams was different as the entry door closed behind him. The overhead lights were off and replaced with something straight out of a dance club, colored flashing and spinning lights and a large complement of black lights.

Walking toward the front counter, he noticed the lanes had phosphorescent arrows on the boards and rope lighting running the length of the gutters.

Dayum! The place knew how to throw a Rock-n-Bowl night, that was for sure.

After his encounter with Candy in the bar the prior Saturday, he decided to give her some space before asking her out again.

As much as she lit a fire inside him, he was here for a very important reason, after all. By all rights, he should just walk away from the temptation completely.

Everything up until now had been about focusing on that brass ring, and it needed to stay that way.

Roping in a small-town cowgirl hadn't been on his to-do list when he got there. Stubborn as he was, though, that didn't mean he wouldn't try.

Candy was behind the front counter checking in customers and smoothly doling out rental shoes.

Sterling got in line behind the last patron and waited his turn. She was good at her job, and it wasn't long before it was his turn at the counter.

Just watching her greet the people at the alley started his heart to gallop. She wasn't just gorgeous. Her personality drew him to her like a stranded man in the desert to an oasis.

She had her back to him as he set his bag on the floor.

"Howdy, beautiful. Got an open lane tonight?"

Candy turned toward him with that same stunning smile he had plastered in his memory.

She wore jeans that looked painted to her amazing curves and a white fitted vest for a top that showed off her tiny waist and ample cleavage with sequins that shined in all the spinning lights.

Sterling caught his breath as he took in the vision before him.

"Didn't expect to see you here tonight." Candy blinked and tossed her hair off one shoulder. "In fact, I was surprised I didn't see you all week."

"Just been keeping my nose to the grindstone, honey." He tipped his hat. "You look amazing."

"I'm sure you say that to all the girls, Sterling." She looked over her clipboard. "But thank you. Not too bad yourself there, cowboy."

"So, how 'bout it? Got a lane for me?"

"You really want a lane? Or you here for some other reason?"

"You wound me." Sterling dramatically put his hand to his chest, covering his heart. "What're you tryin' to say?"

She waved at him. "Knock it off. You're gonna get everybody starin' doin' that. I'll find you a lane."

"Let 'em stare." He shrugged.

"Well, I don't want them starin'. I don't need my business

all out in public." She flipped a page on her clipboard and scanned it with her eyes. "You can have lane eight."

Sterling stood puzzled by her sharp answer. He understood some people were more private than others, but that seemed a little excessive.

He wondered what made her feel that way. "All right then. I didn't mean to upset ya. You workin' all night? Or can you get time off for good behavior?"

"All night, cowboy." She scribbled his name in her ledger and set it on the counter beside her computer.

"Promise me you'll at least stop by and chat later."

"I can't promise you that. I'm workin', ya know."

"Don't make me have to do something crazy to get your attention. Not to mention everybody else in here."

"Oh! You're gonna play that way, huh?" She rested one hand on her hip.

Sterling snugged his hat down on his head, leaned forward over the counter, and locked his gaze with Candy. "I am not above resortin' to actin' a fool to get what I want."

Candy laughed, and Sterling's heart raced at the melodic sound.

"Okay, okay. You win. I'll stop by a bit later."

"I can't ask for much more than that." Sterling bent over to retrieve his bag. "I'll make it worth your while."

"Go bowl, cowboy," Candy replied with a giggle in her voice.

As Sterling set to bowling, his thoughts rarely strayed from Candy. Those bright green eyes, that stunning smile. Oh, and good Lord above, that perfect ass.

If he was going to be honest with himself, the main reason he didn't practice at night was he knew concentration was out of the question with her around. Trying to be polite and not spook the woman were just convenient excuses.

CANDY SAW Sterling the minute he stepped into the line at the counter but refused to let on that she'd spotted him.

Besides, after all her fretting and worrying last Saturday, he hadn't been in even once during her evening shifts all week. After not seeing him, she pretty much figured dinner was off the table, too.

But sweet Jesus, he looked good. His royal blue shirt made his blue eyes sparkle even brighter than usual.

Oh, she played like she wasn't affected by him and was doing a pretty darn good job of it.

That was until he flashed her that gorgeous smile of his, raising her temperature about a thousand degrees and sending shivers up and down her spine.

She fanned herself as she stared at his backside while he walked away. The man was hotter than a summer afternoon in July. It made her weak in the knees and giggle like a silly schoolgirl.

The lane she'd assigned him was close enough for her to see, sure, but it didn't give her the perfect view of his back and legs and ass and— Good Lord, she needed to stop.

Maybe she could swap the folks on lane ten with Sterling. *Like that won't be obvious. Get a grip, girl.* Candy grabbed her coke and took a sip from the straw.

"Candy?"

A hand waved in front of Candy's face, and she jumped before focusing on the man standing before her. *Crap.*

She sighed. "Hey there, Andy. Sorry 'bout that. Caught me daydreamin', I guess." She smoothed her hands down her bare stomach.

"That's all right." Andy raised both brows. "You're lookin' mighty pretty this Saturday night."

"Such a charmer." Candy waved her hand at him. "You look quite nice, too."

Andy owned a ranch about twenty miles outside of town and was a widower. Tall, thickly muscled, and a head full of dark hair with a little gray threaded through it. "Good pickin's," as Trudie would say. Andy was a nice-looking man, no doubt about it.

He'd asked Candy out a few times but finally gave up when she kept turning him down. As nice and good-looking as he was, she couldn't bring herself to date someone local.

She wanted to get out of Strawn, not settle down there.

"I've got you all ready to go on lane seven." Candy checked his name off the list on the clipboard.

"Much obliged." He bent and grabbed his bag. "I think Gilbert'll be comin' in to pair up with me tonight."

"I'll send him over your way when he gets here." She stuck her pen behind her ear. "Have a good game."

Andy walked away from the counter, and Candy rubbed her forehead. She needed to concentrate, and Sterling was already proving to be a big distraction tonight.

The realization that she'd just stuck Andy on the lane next to him was proof of that.

Hell and creation, it was going to be a long night.

Gilbert rolled in ten minutes later, and Candy sent him on his way to lane seven. She crouched down to reorganize the extra shoe stock in preparation for any last-minute customers who might roll in.

"Hey, Candy?"

She looked up to see Sterling peering over the edge of the counter at her and about tumbled back onto her ass. *Double crap!*

"Whoa, sweetheart. Careful now." A look of concern flashed over his face, and he came around the side of the counter and stepped behind it.

Sterling held out his hand for her to take, but feeling like a complete moron, she ignored it.

"Hi." She grimaced, grabbed the counter's edge, and got to her feet. "You needin' somethin'?"

Sterling circled her elbow with his hand, and a sharp zing of arousal ran from her arm through her body. "You okay, Candy?"

"Lost my balance." Her face flushed with heat, and she pulled her arm away. "Go on now, I'm fine. Can't have you back behind the counter."

"I'm sure Mason would understand. But if you're sure you're okay, then I'll scoot." He took a step back.

"Did you need something, or were you just coming by to say hi?"

Sterling walked back around to the customer side of the counter. "Yes, ma'am. Could you move me over to lane seven, if that's okay? I don't have anyone to bowl with, and those gentlemen offered to let me join their group."

Candy raised her brows. "You want to bowl with Andy and Gilbert?"

"Sure. Is that okay? They seem like nice enough fellas."

"No, it's just... Hell." Candy blew out a breath. "Of course, it's okay. You can bowl with anyone you want. I'll make the change on the sheet now."

Lord, the thought of Sterling hanging around with those boys sent her heart into a gallop. What if they told him how she'd refused to go out with Andy?

"Thanks." Sterling stared at her. "You sure you're okay?"

"I'm sure. G'on now, we're about to start." Candy twisted her hands in front of her, then brushed her hair over her shoulders.

He tilted his head to the side. "Still gonna stop by and see me later?" He stood gazing at her.

Like he was studying her every move or something, she felt like a dang bug under a microscope.

"I told you I would." She put her hands on her hips and frowned. "Now scoot."

"You're damn cute when you get all forceful like." Sterling popped his thumbs in his front pockets and rocked on his heels.

The look in his eyes was full of lust and sent a bolt of desire to her clit so fierce the room spun around her as a wave of heat rolled through her. *Dammit.*

Why couldn't she keep control over her lower parts? It wasn't a problem when anyone else flirted with her. But with Sterling, she was fighting a losing battle, and she knew it.

Candy shook her head, and nervous giggles bubbled up and out.

"Your laugh is a melody to my ears, sweetness."

"I'll come visit you after I get everyone rollin'."

"Promise?"

"You don't quit, do you?"

"No, ma'am. Stubborn, I guess." He stepped back from the counter, still facing her, his gaze locked with hers.

Candy rolled her eyes and placed her hand on her hip but shut her mouth to keep from flirting more before she dragged his fine ass back behind the counter and into the office, intent on having her way with his lean body.

How in the heck was she supposed to ignore him tonight?

Chapter Twelve

STERLING WAS HAVING a damn good time.

Everything in his world had been consumed by the desire to get back on top that he'd forgotten what fun it was just to kick back and bowl with a couple of guys.

He never would have guessed that a trip to an out-of-the-way Texas town would be what he needed to return happiness to a game he'd been playing forever.

The small talk was as fast-paced as the game proved to be. Andy and Gilbert could both throw a darn good ball, and they talked like this was the highlight of their week.

Gilbert looked a bit older than Andy, and both were in good shape from manual labor. Just a couple of good ol' boys having a night on the town after a long workweek on the ranch.

Sterling didn't let on about the tournament or his former pro status. He just briefly mentioned that he was in town for a short while before moving on to Fort Worth.

Problem was, even with his newfound bowling buddies, his eyes kept tracking Candy every time she ran by them for one reason or another.

"Ya know, your eyes are gonna pop right outta your head

Dorothy F. Shaw & T. D. Hoffman

if you keep starin' at her like that." Andy motioned toward Candy with his beer bottle in hand.

"Huh? Nah, I ain't starin'. You're up, Gilbert." Sterling sat down in one of the plastic lane chairs.

"Yeah, and the Alamo ain't nuthin' but a fancy name for a strip mall." Gilbert stepped over to the ball return.

"You, too?" Sterling looked around for where he'd set his coke. "Okay, guilty as charged. But cut me some slack. She's pretty."

"I wouldn't waste my time if I were you, buddy." Andy sat across from Sterling as he glanced at the score on the screen above the lane. "Not that I blame you none."

"You tryin' to tell me somethin'?" Sterling wiped the sweat from his forehead.

Sterling watched as Gilbert attempted to pick up his spare, failed, and returned to pick up his beer instead.

"You're up, Andy." Gilbert smacked his friend on the shoulder before taking the seat Andy vacated. "Andy went down that road once." He took a short gulp off his beer bottle.

Gilbert had more than Sterling's attention. The man had every hair on the back of his neck standing up at the thought of somebody else pursuing Candy. "So...they dated?"

"Okay, maybe it was more like *attempted* to go down that road." Gilbert laughed. "She shot him down every time."

Sterling wasn't jealous, but he was a little relieved at the news that she'd never been Andy's girl. *Wait, am I jealous?* The idea of any man with Candy—besides him—got his stomach churning, so yeah, maybe he was.

All the hootin' and hollerin' coming from Andy told Sterling Andy had finally rolled the strike he'd been chasing.

"There ya go!" Sterling cheered, and Gilbert clapped.

"'Bout time! I knew I had at least one more left in me." Andy beamed with excitement. "You're up, Sterling. Beat that."

76

"Gonna be a tough ball to follow." With a wide grin, Sterling stood to take his turn.

Truth be told, he couldn't tell if he was happy for Andy getting his strike or happier for the fact that Candy wouldn't give the guy the time of day.

Sterling took his turn and came up one short of picking up his spare. Usually, it would bother him, but tonight, it didn't seem important.

For reasons he couldn't sort out at that moment, Candy had more of his focus than the game he was attempting to play.

Was Andy not her type? Or had she been playing hard to get? He shook his head to break any unwanted visions of her with another man.

"Damn, that was close, Sterling. Tough spare to pick up." Gilbert ran his fingers through his thinning hair.

"Eh, it's all good. Your turn." Sterling motioned to the lane and then looked between the two men. "You guys want to order some food?"

"Nah, I'm good. Think I'll just stick to my beer tonight." Andy raised his bottle in confirmation.

"You sure? I'm startin' to think nachos might just hit the spot."

"You boys doin' all right over here?" Candy walked up to their area.

Sterling didn't bother hiding the smile that spread across his lips. His heart sped up every time she was close to him and her surprising him just made it worse. "I was just askin' if these guys were hungry. You got this place bugged or somethin'?" Sterling teased Candy. "Or do you just have perfect timin'?"

"My mama always said timin' was everything." She clapped her hands together. "What'll it be? Another round?"

Timing *was* everything, good and bad.

Sterling had come to town to fine-tune his game and put himself in the best possible position to reclaim his pro status.

With only three weeks to go until the big day, he found his head more and more consumed with thoughts of this little bombshell on a daily basis.

Andy and Gilbert agreed on more drinks while Sterling ordered nachos and a regular coke. Gilbert started toward the ball return for his turn, and Andy swallowed the last of the golden liquid in his bottle before setting it back on the table.

"All right, boys, I'll get your order in for you." Candy eyed Sterling. "Take it easy on these guys, will ya."

"Since it's you askin', I'll definitely give it some good consideration." Lust filled Sterling's veins as the sight of the multicolored lights dancing over her body became etched in his memory.

"Oh dang, I forgot. The kitchen's closed tonight, cowboy. I'm sorry; Danny had to leave early for somethin' important."

"Well, shucks, I was really hopin' for somethin' tasty tonight." Sterling looked her up and down and licked his lips. "What's a cowboy to do?"

Candy shifted her weight to one foot, planted a hand on her hip and stared at Sterling with a blank look on her face.

Hmm. He stepped toward his seat. "Tell ya what, let me know if anything changes."

"Yeah, I'll do that." Candy turned to head for the bar. "I'll grab the drinks for y'all," she hollered over her shoulder.

Sterling stopped short of saying what was really on his mind, that he wished she were on the menu. He figured he certainly wouldn't score any points with her, being that forward, especially in front of an audience.

"What the hell'd you say to her?" Gilbert asked.

"What are you talkin' about?"

"I was over there, remember?" Gilbert pointed to the lane. "When I turned, Candy had this look on her face—"

"I didn't say anything, just that I was hungry," Sterling said.

"It's true. One minute, he's ordering food. The next, she just stared at him," Andy joined in.

"All I know is, I've never seen her speechless before." Gilbert sat down next to Andy. "You musta said somethin'. Andy, your turn."

"Let's just bowl, guys. Drinks'll be here in a minute."

CANDY WALKED AWAY from Sterling and the guys as fast as her booted feet could take her.

The man still had a look in his eyes like he was ready to make a meal out of her, and if she didn't get away from him right quick, she might not stop him.

And Andy had watched the whole dang thing. How in the heck was she going to handle this? God, she should've let the regular floor server handle their orders.

One more hour, just one more hour, and she'd be home. In her bed. Alone.

Alone.

Why did that thought disappoint her instead of making her feel relieved?

Candy stood at the bar service window for their refills and rested her chin on her clenched fist.

"Hey, sugar. Whatcha needin'?" Trudie pulled a beer out of the cooler and popped the cap.

"Two more Buds and a regular coke."

"Sure thing. I'm assumin' this is for Sterling and gang." Trudie delivered the beer she was holding and pulled two more from the cooler. "Did he ask ya to dinner again?" She set the beers down in front of Candy.

"No." Candy sighed. "But he's hintin' around it for sure."

"Child, you have just got me baffled. Fine pickin' like that, and you're avoidin' him like the plague." Trudie placed the coke on the counter next to the beers.

"I don't want to talk about it." Candy grabbed the two bottles in one hand and the glass in the other and stepped away from the window.

"You been sayin' that all week!" Trudie hollered after her.

Candy ignored her and kept walking.

Trudie had been hounding her all week about Sterling. The woman was like a dog with a bone. Once she had hold of something, there was no letting it go.

Candy would have to tell her eventually. Maybe she could manage not to let it out until after Sterling was gone. She groaned at the thought of having to fight off Trudie for another three weeks.

When she approached lane seven, Sterling was bowling his turn. She set the drinks down and watched his approach— serious, thoughtful movements, just like she'd watched him do last week.

She glanced up at the score monitors. He was kicking their butts.

"You seem a little out of sorts tonight, Miss Candy." Gilbert handed her a twenty for their drinks.

"Do I? Don't mind me, I'm just tired." She counted out his change.

"Night's almost done now. You get on home and get some rest, ya hear me?"

"I plan on it. No need to worry over me."

Sterling turned and faced her.

Their gazes locked.

She sighed as a wave of craving rolled through from her feet to her head and back down again.

Sweet Lord in Heaven, she wanted him.

Her head might be screaming at her to run in the other

direction, but her body didn't give one damn what her head wanted. Her body wanted Sterling. Plain and simple.

She shook her head as a slow smile spread across her mouth, and she turned and walked away, making sure to put a little more swing in her hips than usual.

Playin' with fire, Candy girl. It was risky, and she'd probably be burned in the end, but the thought of having him between her legs again won out over every argument her mind was making.

STERLING TRACKED every sway of Candy's hips as she walked away.

Desire burned in his gut, and he had to mentally force his head not to sway back and forth right along with her.

Damn, that woman had him wrapped up good. Every sharp response from her just drove his desire for her higher. A wink from her and a flash of her smile rendered him incapable of rational thought.

He wanted another night with her, no doubt about it. Maybe several if he could.

He turned and looked at the scoreboard above, noting the time and number of frames left in their game.

"Come on, boys, let's get her wrapped up. Less than an hour before they're gonna be kickin' us outta here." Sterling looked over at Gilbert, who was looking a little pie-eyed. "Well, they might be rollin' you outta here." He chuckled.

Andy started laughing at the jab and slapped his buddy on the shoulder. "How many lanes you seein'?"

"Ah hell, I'm just gettin' started on my buzz. I ain't thrown my ball down the wrong lane yet." Gilbert took another quick swallow off his beer bottle.

Dorothy F. Shaw & T. D. Hoffman

They finished their game and another round of drinks before the main lights came on, signifying closing time.

The jabs and jokes continued throughout, and everyone kept smiling. Sterling liked these guys and wouldn't mind bowling with them again if the opportunity came up.

Andy invited Sterling to stop by his ranch sometime while he was still in town and then headed for the parking lot with Gilbert, promising to drive him home and come back for Gilbert's truck tomorrow.

As the remaining customers exited, Sterling packed up his bag. When he bent to put his boots back on, Candy stepped in front of where he was leaning over.

His eyes memorized every inch and every curve of her sexy little body as he took his sweet time raising his gaze to meet hers. Sterling blew out a long breath. "I don't think I could ever get tired of lookin' at you."

"I swear, you must have a million lines stored up in that head of yours."

"That ain't no line, Candy. Just speakin' the truth." He loved that she always had a comment waiting for him.

She was way more than a pretty girl in barely there clothes, and damn if that didn't make her even more exciting.

Candy paused for a second as her cheeks flushed pink. "Well, in that case, thank you, cowboy. She winked and ran her fingers through the length of hair draped over one shoulder. "You're probably still full of it, but I'll let it slide this time."

Sterling chuckled. "So how 'bout it? Any good places to eat this late? I'm hungry as all get out." He zipped up the pockets of his bag. "I certainly wouldn't mind the company if you're interested in joinin' me. It'd sure make *my* day."

Candy laughed and looked around the bowling alley before sitting down across from Sterling. "I'm sorry the kitchen was closed tonight."

"No need to apologize." Sterling tilted his head to the side.

"But if you really want to make it up to me, just say yes to joinin' me."

"Not much open this time of night, but I've got eggs and sausage at my place if you're interested." She stood and smoothed out her form-fitting jeans, running her hands down the front of her thighs.

"Damn right, I am." He rose and pulled her into his arms, wrapping them around her. He bent his head, and the air seemed to charge with electricity before his lips found their target.

She wrapped her arms around Sterling's neck as he kissed her with deep passion.

Her hips pressed to his, her skin heating everywhere he touched her. Pulling her tight to his chest, he turned and pressed her body between his and the half wall.

He smoothed his hands up and down the length of her waist before cupping her luscious ass to the sound of her soft moans.

"Not fair, cowboy."

"Nope." He kissed her again, reinforcing his draw to her. "You got room for this old pro in that bed of yours?"

"Mmm." She pulled away and raised a single brow. "I'll consider it. Grab your stuff, let's get outta here."

Chapter Thirteen

CANDY DROVE the winding back roads in silence toward her little single-wide trailer with Sterling following behind her.

Her mind replayed the heat between them before they'd left and then retraced, yet again, the night she'd spent with him at Bowling Dreams.

As she pulled into her narrow gravel driveway, Candy decided, with a deep sigh, that what was done was done.

She didn't want everyone in the town knowing, but she'd be stupid not to enjoy the rest of her time with this cowboy. Have fun, then send him off at the end of the month with a sweet kiss and a good luck wish.

Sterling held the front door open for her. "Quiet out here."

"Sure is. Too quiet." Candy set her stuff on the little table when they entered and walked toward the kitchen. "Scrambled or fried?"

"Scrambled works just fine, thank you kindly. Nice place you got yourself here."

"Thanks. It's small, and as much as I'd love to get outta here, it's home."

It was a little strange, but kind of exciting, having a man in her home again. There hadn't been since Jared had left her.

Candy shook her head to clear the thoughts of her ex away and set to cooking them a meal. She sure didn't need her mood spoiled with thoughts of Jared.

"Can I help? I'm pretty good in the kitchen."

Shit fire and save the matches. Could the man get any more perfect? Handsome as could be, great body, fantastic lover, *and* he cooked?

Candy frowned and rubbed her forehead as her mind raced in circles, trying to make sense of how this man had ended up in her life.

Coming up short, Candy looked over at him. "Where in the *hell* did you come from?"

"Uh...Las Cruces?" Stepping toward the cabinets, he opened one of the doors. "Plates up in here?"

"Not exactly what I meant." She sighed and opened the correct cabinet for him.

"Oookay. What did you mean then?"

Candy shook her head at his innocent expression. Did he really not get it? And the look on his face made him all the more appealing.

"Never mind me, I'm just tired." She hooked her thumbs in her back pockets. "This is about done. Could you dish it up? I'm gonna change into some jammies, if you don't mind."

"Not at all. You go right ahead. I got this." He leaned and kissed her cheek.

Sheesh, this had to be some sort of cruel joke. Did God just plop this man in her lap, only for him to be gone in less than a month? *Figures.*

Hopelessness settled hard like a boulder in Candy's gut as she pulled off her clothes and grabbed a pair of pink yoga pants and a fitted tank top.

Enjoy him while I got him, remember? Pulling her long hair into a ponytail, she scurried back to the kitchen.

Sterling sat at the table, two plates full of eggs and sausage steaming before him and two full glasses of milk.

He whistled low as he stood and pulled a chair out for her. "Like an angel from above, you make anything look good."

"Your blood sugar might be low." She felt her cheeks get warm and sat down. "Thank you," she mumbled, remembering her manners, and focused on her plate.

Dang, could he get any sweeter?

"Guess I'm in luck then. You can replenish me after we eat." He grinned. "Besides, it's true, you're cuter than a speckled pup under a red wagon."

She snorted and almost choked on the first bite she'd just forked into her mouth.

"Easy now." He patted her back. "Although I am certified in mouth-to-mouth if needed."

She wiped her mouth with her napkin in an attempt to compose herself. "You and them one-liners."

"I prefer to think of 'em as creative statements."

"Nice." She rolled her eyes and laughed. He was just too cute *and* clever. The easy back-and-forth between them helped wash away her sadness.

They set to eating their meal, chitchatting between bites. When they'd almost finished, he asked, "Have you always lived in Strawn?"

"No. Moved here from Abilene just outta high school."

"Big city compared to Strawn. Why here?"

She took a sip of her milk. "Chasin' a boy." She shrugged. "My high school sweetheart, Jared. I swear my life is like a country song."

And here she was, adding to it. In less than a month's time, Sterling would be gone. The thought loomed in her mind like a summer storm cloud.

But did she really have anything to lose by opening up to him? She wasn't sure. *Enjoy him. Sheesh!* At least being away from prying eyes made it easier.

"Mine, too." He leaned back in his chair. "Care to share what happened?"

"You wouldn't believe me if I told ya." Smirking, Candy took a bite of her eggs. She could give as good as he could.

"Ah, touché. All right then, let's play a little game." He clapped his hands and rubbed them together. "Question for question?"

"Deal, but I'm goin' first." She moved her plate aside. "And you have to answer every question truthfully. No sand-baggin'." She wagged her finger at him.

"Never." He took a swallow of his milk.

"How'd you *really* hurt your shoulder?"

He pushed his plate aside and leaned forward, crossing his forearms on the table. "I told you already."

"For real? A mechanical bull?" She narrowed her eyes. Candy wasn't settling for the same lines this time. This had to be a big old oozing sore as far as she was concerned. "Details, cowboy."

"If you insist." He sighed. "Me and a few friends went out one night after one of the pro-tour games. We were all drinkin' way too much, and this dude bet me I couldn't stay on the bull longer than him." He shrugged. "I won."

"But the shoulder?"

"Tore my rotator cuff holdin' on for dear life."

"Dang." She blew out a breath. The man had lost his entire career in a matter of minutes. No wonder he told it like he did. "How long ago did this happen?"

"About—" He paused, tipping his head to the side. "—Nine years, three surgeries, and months of excruciatingly painful physical therapy ago."

She studied him a moment. "Bless your heart, that must've been really hard to go through. That's why you make a joke about it, huh?"

"Pretty much. I was a kid and screwed up my ride. There

ain't no point in sharing the meat of it with people. Besides, I'm past all that now."

"I admire your drive. Lots of people would've given up."

"More like bein' a stubborn ass, but thanks." He ran his palm over his short hair.

"That's why you don't drink, then?"

"Yup. Been a sober member of AA ever since."

"You haven't had a drink in nine years? I don't know anyone who doesn't drink. You went through so much. That's really amazing."

"The way I figure it, drinkin' hadn't brought me nothin' good. Cost me my dream, so I gave it up. The AA program saved my life. With the Twelve Steps and a good sponsor, I cleared out a herd of demons."

Candy had never known anyone like him in her life. He'd picked himself up and changed for the better.

Sitting back in her seat, she gazed over at him. *Less than a month.* How was it he was still single? She could fall in love with a man like him. *Dang, this is so unfair.*

"I do believe it's your turn, ma'am." He propped his chin on his fist.

"Knew that was comin'."

"What happened with Jared?"

Candy blew out a breath and decided to give him the whole story since he'd just shared his with her. "Like I said, we were high school sweethearts. My momma hated him, though. Said he'd ruin me. She was right."

"You don't look ruined to me."

"Ha. Maybe, maybe not. I was a curious young girl with stars in my eyes, and I ran away with him, then I married him." She shook her head. "We landed here for some grain mill job that he lost a short time later. After that, it was odd jobs here and there and gamblin' debts he'd racked up at a casino in Oklahoma. Fights in town. Gettin' arrested and thrown in jail, so on and so forth."

"How long were y'all married?"

"Too. Dang. Long." She groaned and dropped her head in her hands. "Nine years before he skipped bail, then town," she mumbled.

Sterling pulled her hands away from her face and held them in his own. "How long ago?"

"Over two years ago. Bastard left me with a ton of debt, too. I filed for divorce a little while later when I realized he wasn't coming back." Candy met his gaze. "Just grateful we never had any babies."

The feel of his warm, calloused palms kick-started the memory of them on her skin last week. He'd touched her everywhere, and her body hummed at the thought. Lord help her, she wanted him again.

"Yeah, that woulda made it a lot harder, I imagine. Why didn't you head back home?"

Pulling her hands away, Candy stood and gathered their plates. "Nothin' to go home to. Momma passed away five years ago, and my daddy was gone before I was outta diapers." She set the dirty dishes in the sink. "Besides, like I said, Momma was right. Even if she hadn't passed away, I woulda been too ashamed to show my face back there anyway."

Boy howdy, she was letting it all hang out now. Candy heard the chair scrape on the linoleum floor when he stood.

"Wow, your life *is* like a country song." He leaned against the counter next to her and grinned.

She snorted. "I tried to warn ya. What about you? You ever been married? Kids?"

"Let me do that." Scooting her to the side, he started washing their dishes.

It took Candy a second to drag herself together from the shock of his offer before she pulled a clean towel from the drawer to dry as he washed.

She liked how he looked in her kitchen. She liked that he wanted to help, too. She liked it a lot.

Sterling handed her a wet dish. "Nope, never got hitched. No kids either. As far as I know, anyway."

"As far as you know, huh?" Candy smirked.

"You and I are pretty dang similar if you think about it."

"How's that?"

"We both lost a dream, suffered for nine long years getting through it, and then there's that whole stubborn ass thing, or as you nicely phrased it: 'drive.'"

She groaned at how sweet he was. "I think the stubborn ass description might be more accurate. But I guess you have a point. Though you're gonna get your dream back, I don't want Jared back. I quit that job."

"I'm *hoping* to get my dream back, and I'll give my all. And hell, I know you're too stubborn to take that fool back now." Leaning over, he stole a kiss. "Mmm, I like how stubborn tastes."

She nodded. "You're right. We are pretty similar." Licking her lips, she gazed up at him. "I like how you're stubborn tastes, too."

"Guess it's settled then." With the dishes finished, Sterling took her hand and led her to her bedroom. When they got into her dark room, he turned toward her and kissed her, stroking her face with his large hands. "There ain't nothin' ruined about you, darlin'."

Candy melted into a puddle of goo at the sweetness of his words.

He was so dang tall compared to her, and it made her feel like she was tiny as could be. Rising on tiptoe, she hooked her arms around his neck and touched her mouth to his again.

With a low growl, Sterling scooped her up in his arms, laid her down on her bed, and then peeled off her clothes.

He straightened and took off his shirt. Unbuttoning his

jeans, he slid them, along with his boxers, down his narrow hips and removed them.

As Candy focused on his erection, hard and thick, angling up and away from his groin, she licked her lips, remembering the taste of him from the week prior. *My God, he's beautiful.*

He gripped his length, stroked himself, then cupped his heavy sac in his palm before bending and pulling a condom from his pants pocket.

After rolling it on, he laid down beside her.

Chapter Fourteen

As STERLING DIPPED HIS HEAD, searching for her lips, he ran his hand over her stomach and rested it on her hip.

The kiss started gentle, then grew heated as Candy responded to his touch.

Tasting her lips with his tongue, she opened for him.

With a moan, she smoothed her hands up his chest and around his neck and then laid one leg over his hip.

Breaking the kiss, Sterling pulled back to gaze at her. "My Lord, woman. You are gorgeous."

"Come on now." She sighed. "You've been around. I'm sure you've seen plenty of women."

"I'm very serious, Candy. You're beautiful."

"I *was* seri—"

Sterling cut off her reply with a well-timed kiss, rolling his body on top of hers as her legs wrapped around his hips. He trailed kisses down her neck and collarbone to her pert nipple, drawing slow circles with his tongue around the tight peak before sucking it into his mouth.

Gasping, Candy arched her back off the bed and grabbed the back of his head with one hand, holding him to her.

He squeezed her other breast and teased her nipple with

his thumb. Nipping his way between her cleavage, he tasted her skin as he began inching down her belly.

"Where do you think you're going, cowboy?"

"I need to taste my Candy." Sterling gazed up at her.

"Next time."

"You're gonna *deny* my sweet tooth?"

"I need you inside me. Now." Candy dug her heels into his ass and pulled him closer.

"Damn, honey." He groaned. "Since you put it that way." He sat up on his knees and palmed his throbbing erection, guiding it to part her slick folds. "So wet for me, baby. Mmm."

"Stop teasing me," she groaned.

He entered her slowly, pressing inside her hot core. Pushing her thighs wide, he moved deeper.

"Yes." Candy's head rolled back as she gasped.

"You feel so good wrapped around me."

She rolled her pelvis to accept all of him as their hips met.

Sterling leaned in and kissed her hard, their tongues wrestling as he began to thrust in and out of her slick pussy.

Candy wrapped her arms around his back and dug her nails into his skin as their rhythm intensified. Her thighs flexed around his hips as she pulled him deeper within her.

"Oh God, Sterling, yes…" She arched into him.

He thrust harder, his release building. As he slid in and out of her, their skin slapped together in time with their moans.

His muscles tightened, and the feel of her nails scratching down his back was about to send him over the edge.

"I'm so close, cowboy." Candy's breathing grew heavy. "Come with me."

Sterling was past the point of no return as his release flooded through him, and he drove deep inside her one more time.

Candy's arms and legs tightened around his body as her breath hitched. Then, every muscle in her body relaxed as Sterling collapsed against her, their breathing heavy in unison.

Sterling kissed her neck and rolled to his back, bringing Candy to rest on top of him.

CANDY SHIFTED to the side to lie on the bed next to Sterling and nestled her head on his chest. Her heart finally calmed to a slower beat.

He trailed his calloused fingers up and down her back, and she curled closer to him.

"That was one heck of a ride, cowboy." She yawned.

"Glad you liked it."

"Mm-hmm." She kissed his chest.

"Gonna run to the bathroom, sweetheart. You need anything while I'm up?"

"Water would be nice."

"Comin' right up." Sterling kissed her forehead and got to his feet.

Candy gathered the blankets that had settled at the foot of the bed and pulled them over herself. She should really grab a nightie from her drawer and probably use the bathroom, too, but she was too tired to bother.

The toilet flushed, and she heard the bathroom door open, then Sterling's footsteps in the hall. A few minutes later, he returned to her room with a tall glass of water.

She sat up and took the cool drink from him. "Thank you." She tipped the glass back, swallowed a big gulp, and handed it back to him.

Sterling set it on the night table and climbed back into her bed.

"Are you sleeping over?" She lay back down.

"If that's all right with you." Sterling fluffed the pillow and lay down.

"Well, I guess. I just…" Candy shrugged. "It's fine."

"It's pretty late. You really want to send me on my way?"

"No. It's okay." Candy scooted closer to him.

Sterling turned to face her. "You sure?" He ran his fingers through her hair.

Candy nodded and closed her eyes. She *did* want him to stay but worried about her neighbors seeing a strange truck in her driveway. Maybe no one would be around by the time he left in the morning. She hated people knowing her business.

"You're frowning."

Candy opened her eyes. "Am not."

Sterling ran his fingers over her brow. "You sure are. What's on your mind, babe?"

Candy turned over and scooted her bottom against his groin. Lord knew she had no poker face at all, so it was best he not be able to see any signs of her worry.

Sterling wrapped an arm around her waist and pulled her tight against his chest. "C'mon now, spill it."

"You wore me out, cowboy. Don't go lettin' it go to your head, though." She lied and wiggled her hips a bit, hoping to distract him. "I'm just tired."

"I'll wait until tomorrow morning to pound my chest like a caveman." Sterling nipped her shoulder. "Sleep, sweetheart. You wore me out, too."

Candy let out a deep sigh and entwined her fingers with his. She liked how he felt spooned up behind her. He was a big man, yet fit right against her like he'd been made to be there.

And the sex? Lord, the sex was incredible. Again.

Candy closed her eyes with thoughts of how good Sterling had felt when he sank deep inside her. And thoughts of how many times she might get to feel that again over the next few weeks.

The hard part was going to be not letting him sink into her heart, too.

Chapter Fifteen

THE NEXT MORNING, Sterling woke on his back to find Candy nuzzled into his chest. Still asleep, she had one leg draped over his and an arm around his waist.

He really hadn't expected all this. He'd come to town to practice before moving on. Sterling certainly hadn't planned on meeting anybody, let alone someone like Candy.

Not that he was complaining. The woman lit a fire in him every time he was near her. Frankly, he couldn't find anything he didn't like yet.

As far as he was concerned, he planned to spend as much time as he could with her while he was in town. There was no reason to avoid it as long as he didn't lose focus on his main goal, Fort Worth.

Candy stirred against him, stretching as she yawned, then rubbed the sleep from her eyes before looking up at him.

"G'mornin', sunshine." He rubbed her warm back.

"Mornin'. What time is it?"

"Not sure. I haven't checked yet. Just woke a minute ago myself."

Candy rolled away from him enough to check the clock on

her nightstand, then sat up. "Dangit, it's already eleven o'clock."

"I don't know 'bout you, but I slept pretty damn hard."

"Guess we really did wear each other out." Candy brushed her hair out of her face with her fingers, scratching her head a bit as she did.

"Hey, I got an idea." He pulled her back down to rest her head on his chest. "Whaddya say we get dressed and head into town for some late breakfast?"

"No." She sat back up. "I mean, I really don't feel like a late breakfast right now."

"Okay. We can call it an early lunch if you like instead."

"Really, I think I just want to lounge around this mornin'. Besides, I have food here."

Sterling pushed himself up, sat against the headboard and laced his fingers together behind his head.

"That's fine by me if that's what you wanna do. I was just thinkin' less dishes."

"Never heard of paper plates?" She patted his chest, teasing him. "Lemme throw some clothes on, and I'll see what's in the fridge."

Candy rose out of bed and grabbed her yoga pants off the floor.

"Don't go gettin' all fancied up for me, darlin'. I'm fine with what ya got on."

"I just bet you are." She snorted a laugh. "Now, where is my tank top?"

Sterling tossed off the covers and dropped his legs over the edge of the bed. He paused and rubbed his shoulder while he scanned the floor for his jeans.

Spotting them, he scooped them up and pulled them on, buttoning them as he stood.

Candy found her top and then pulled her long, slightly tangled sex hair up in a tie. "Anything you're in the mood for?"

"Now that you mention it—" He pulled her into an embrace. "—I could think of a few things."

"Oh, no you don't, cowboy." She placed a hand on his chest to stop him from going farther. "Two words: morning breath. You best let me brush my teeth first."

"Ha. Yeah, me, too." He chuckled and released his hold on her.

As Sterling returned from the bathroom, a delicious scent from the kitchen greeted him while Candy set paper plates and silverware on the table.

"Dayum, that smells good. Is that French toast?"

"Seemed like a good idea this mornin'. I hope you like it."

"I love it already and haven't even tasted it." Remembering his manners, he paused before pulling out his chair. "You need any help?"

"Nah, I got it." Candy placed the plate with a tall stack of French toast in the center of the table. "You could grab the coffee if you want."

"Sure thing."

He grabbed two cups, filled them, and returned to the table.

Candy headed for the shower after breakfast, leaving Sterling in the kitchen to do the dishes.

She'd never met a man so willing to help out as he was. It made her wonder if it was all for show—people tended to be on their best behavior when getting to know someone, after all.

But based on what she had learned so far about Sterling Day, he was the real deal. *Guess his momma raised him right.*

After tossing on a fresh pair of yoga pants and matching

tank top, Candy added a light touch of makeup and pulled the crown of her long hair into a clip.

She stepped from the bathroom and stopped short when she heard a familiar female voice. Hell and damnation, it was Sunday, and she'd forgotten.

Candy turned and pressed her forehead against the wall. *Lord Jesus, get me outta this mess, please?*

After a couple of deep breaths, she made her way down the remainder of the hall and peeked around the corner.

Trudie sat on the couch, one leg tucked under her, the other crossed over the other, her slip-on high heel dangling as she bounced her foot.

Today, she wore a bright orange blouse and purple leggings with orange polka dots on them.

Good Lord, the woman was a fashion nightmare, but she always made it work.

Sterling sat beside her, quiet as a mouse, while Trudie rattled on about God knows what.

Deep breath, girl. Just go on in there and act normal.

Candy stepped into the kitchen. "Hey, Trudie. I wasn't expectin' you."

"Weren't expectin' me?" Trudie gaped. "Darlin', we made plans on Thursday for today. How could you forget?" Trudie frowned.

"I..." Candy crossed her arms. *Crap.* "I got distracted, I guess." Candy reached into the fridge and grabbed a sports drink.

"Hard not to be with Sterling making your couch look so nice and all."

Sterling laughed. "Now, Miss Trudie, stop that. You're gonna make me blush."

"But it's true. Did she let you take her to dinner yet?"

"No, ma'am, she hasn't."

"Hello! I'm right here, y'all." Candy shook her head and sat in the chair across from them.

"You keep tryin', cowboy. Eventually, she'll give in." Trudie studied her nails.

Candy rolled her eyes and took a swig of her drink.

Did Sterling tell Trudie he'd spent the night? No. He wouldn't have done that. He was too much of a gentleman to kiss and tell.

She hoped anyway.

"We were just about to watch a movie. Did you care to join us, Miss Trudie? I sure didn't mean to intrude on your time with Candy."

"We were?" Candy looked at Sterling, and he winked at her. "I mean, we were." She set her drink down and coughed. "Yes, Trudie, you're welcome to stay." *Crap, crap, crap. Please say no.*

Trudie pursed her lips and tilted her head to the side. "Sugar, I think it's best I make myself scarce. Give you two a little cuddle time." She stood. "We can go shoe shopping anytime."

Candy jumped up. "We're not...it's not what you...Ugh. I don't want the whole town knowin', Trudie."

Trudie made the motion, showing her lips were locked up tight. "Don't worry, sugar. I won't say a word."

Candy knew better, though. Trudie might be the closest thing to a best friend she had here, but that wouldn't stop her from blabbing.

All of Strawn would know that Sterling was on Candy's couch before the sun rose tomorrow morning.

Trudie gave Candy a peck on the cheek and made her way to the door. Pausing, she looked back at Sterling. "Remember what I said, Sterling."

"Yes, ma'am." Sterling stood.

"Quit calling me ma'am. Startin' to make me feel old, and believe me, you, cowboy, I've got plenty of young left in this body." Trudie shifted her hips from side to side and fluffed her hair.

Candy slapped her forehead and cringed. "Thanks for the mental image."

"Sugar, it tickles me to no end how embarrassed you get." Trudie winked at Candy's and then walked out the door.

Candy turned to Sterling. "I'm sorry. I forgot I'd made plans."

"I got no problem with it. I feel kinda bad, actually. You sure you don't want to call her back?" He stepped in front of her and pulled her into his arms. "I can go if you want." He bent his head and kissed her.

Candy rose on tiptoe and took what he gave. The man had a way with his tongue. It made her belly tighten, and her knees go weak every time he kissed her.

Actually, he had many ways with his tongue, and she liked all of them—quite a bit.

Sterling nipped at her bottom lip, then her upper one, taking little sips of kisses in between before pulling away.

She sighed and gazed up at him.

"You ready for that movie now?"

"Lead the way, cowboy. I'm all yours."

Chapter Sixteen

THE WEEK HAD GONE WELL. Sterling practiced hard most every day and found that texts and phone calls between him and Candy gave him an extra energy boost to push harder through the afternoons.

Every time he heard her voice, his heart pounded out of his chest, and he couldn't wait to tell her how much stronger and more consistently he was bowling.

Sterling packed away his gear for lunch, figuring on returning for a few more frames in a couple hours, when Andy walked up to the half wall between them.

"Hey, Sterling, how's things?"

Sterling straightened and walked over to shake his hand. "Howdy, Andy, good to see you."

"Heard you were training for the tourney in Fort Worth. How come you didn't say nuthin' last weekend?"

"Didn't figure it was all that important right then. Just wanted to have a good time instead of work, work, work." Sterling set his bag on the half wall.

"Yeah, that makes sense to me. Speaking of a good time, if you ain't doin' nuthin' tonight, you should come out to my ranch. The hands are talkin' 'bout a poker game."

"Well, that's awful nice of you to invite me along." Sterling reached into the side pocket of his bag and retrieved a sucker. "Think I can get a rain check?" He unwrapped the lollipop and put it in his mouth.

"That's a shame." Andy's brow creased, and he appeared disappointed. "I was hopin' you might make it."

"I really do appreciate it, Andy. I just try hard not to do much during the week. Practice schedule and all." He turned, grabbed his hat off one of the seats, and came right back.

"I suppose that makes sense, too. I thought maybe you had a hot date or somethin' instead."

"What in the world would give you that idea?"

"Word on the town is you and Candy are a hot ticket these days." Andy grinned like a cat that'd just caught a bird.

"Seriously?" Suspicion rose in his gut, and he frowned at Andy's remark. "Is that what brought you down here? To see if there was any truth to it?"

"Okay, guilty. You caught me."

"That's pretty messed up." Sterling rubbed his hand over the back of his neck. "And poker tonight? More investigating?"

"Don't take it like that. I'm not tryin' to be rude." Andy looked down at his feet and then back to Sterling. "It's just kind of curious, is all. I mean, pro bowler breezes through town and charms local small-town woman? She may have turned me down, but she's a sweet girl. She don't deserve to be hurt by anyone."

"I'm here to practice. I'm here to go pro again." He shifted his weight to one foot. "And I'm not all too happy at the prospect of people talkin' 'bout me like that. Not to mention, it ain't fair to Candy one bit. That ain't right, and you know it."

"No, no. I suppose you're right. I was just hopin' that since we all had a good time on Saturday, maybe you might fill me in."

"Fill you in on what?"

"You and Candy, of course."

"Andy, I'm only gonna say this one more time. I'm here to practice for my tournament."

"Well, that ain't much of an answer." Andy shrugged.

"Don't push it. There's nuthin' to answer 'cause it ain't nobody's business."

"Hey, now, I'm sorry." Andy put his hands up in defense. "I really didn't mean no offense."

"Then can we drop it?"

"Yeah, yeah. You're right. None of my business anyway." Andy put his hand out to shake. "No hard feelin's?"

"As long as it's a dead topic, yeah. No hard feelings." Sterling grasped the man's hand and shook it.

"Fair enough. Plus, I'd still like to bowl with you again sometime." Andy shrugged. "Gives me stories to tell. Ya know, 'I used to bowl with Sterling Day' stories."

"We can bowl." Sterling put his hands in his pockets. "And bring Gilbert along, too."

"Thanks. Maybe we can run into you this weekend again." Andy waved as he turned.

"Sounds like a plan. See ya later."

Wow. Did that just happen? Sterling definitely *did not* know what to expect in this town.

In Las Cruces, people minded their own business. Everyone had their own lives to deal with, no time for cluttering it up with others business.

He watched as Andy exited through the glass doors at the end of the alley.

Sterling reached for his phone in his back pocket and hit the keys with his thumb.

Sterling: You're not gonna believe what just happened. Apparently, we are the talk of the town.

He hit send, gathered his hat and bag, and started for the door. Sterling hoped Candy wouldn't be too upset, but somehow, he knew that wouldn't be the case.

His phone beeped, and he looked at the screen.

> Candy: Excuse me?! Dammit Trudie!

Sterling paused for a moment, then replied.

> Sterling: This is Sterling, darlin, not Trudie.

All else fails, go with humor. Sterling hit send and kept walking through the doors and out to his car.

CANDY WAS ABOUT to walk out the door to get her nails and toes done when she read the text from Sterling.

And now, she was furious and not going anywhere. She knew Trudie would blab, and even though her friend had promised not to, Candy should have known better than to trust her.

She got another text from Sterling but ignored it and sent one to Trudie.

> Candy: Dang it, Trudie! Who'd you tell?

> Trudie: Sugar, what in the Lord's name are you talkin' bout?

> Candy: You know exactly what I'm talkin about. Me and Sterling? You said you weren't gonna tell!

Trudie: I didn't. Oh, wait. Well, hell. I told Billy, but he swore he wouldn't say nuthin.

Candy: You promised! You know I don't need to be the talk of the town. Again. How am I supposed to deal with this when he leaves?

Trudie: I'm sorry, sugar. I'll talk to Billy and see who he told. See if I can fix it or somethin. I'll try, sweetheart.

Candy: Fine. But I'm still mad at you.

Trudie: I'll see you tonight and you can yell at me some more. I earned it.

Candy didn't bother replying to Trudie's last text.

She checked the message from Sterling that she'd not read yet. *Very funny, cowboy. I ain't responding to you either.*

The only call she made was to Mason, calling in sick to work.

She needed to figure out how in the heck she was going to weather this storm. Candy wasn't ready to deal with any of it today.

Tossing her phone aside, she went and took a long hot bath.

Throughout the night, her phone beeped with text messages from Sterling and a few from Trudie. She ignored all of them.

She'd deal with the two of them tomorrow, as well as the prying questions and knowing looks from the customers at the alley.

For tonight, she'd just do as she pleased, which included giving herself a pretty decent mani and pedi.

It saved her forty bucks, and that was always a good thing. She watched some old reruns of *Family Guy*, ate popcorn, and relaxed.

Chapter Seventeen

By Friday afternoon, Candy was determined not to see Sterling again. He was only going to be here a couple more weeks anyway.

One way to stop the rumor mill was to give them nothing to talk about.

Scooping up a pile of mail from the counter, she sorted through it, tearing the junk mail in half and tossing it in the trash as frustration burned through her.

She'd been the subject of gossip one too many times already in this one-horse town. She sure as heck didn't need to go through it again.

What she needed was to focus on getting her bills paid and getting her hind end out of this tiny town. She grabbed the pile she'd sorted and tossed it on the kitchen table. She was too annoyed to deal with any of it.

Screwing some bowler on his way back to pro status was not on her to-do list. Sure, it was fun while it lasted, and she did like him—a lot—but it was time to end it.

One little affair wasn't worth going back to being the town's hot topic. She should've known better and never let him back in her bed.

Candy dropped her hands in her head as the anger burning in her belly turned to confusion. It'd been so good with him that she just couldn't help herself. Maybe she should—

No. She was done.

She had to be.

Subject closed.

THE COLD SHOULDER? Really? Sterling thought he'd had something good starting up with Candy. He wasn't so sure anymore.

Of course, Fort Worth still took the number one spot on his priority list, but the "shutout" was beginning to bother him a bit more than he'd expected.

They'd gone from daily texting and long phone calls to no contact—stone-cold silence.

As he shouldered his bag from another long day of practice, his stomach reminded him that dinnertime was rapidly approaching.

After dropping his stuff in his hotel room, he headed off to the nearest restaurant. Not like there was a whole lot to choose from in this town.

After he was instructed to sit anywhere he wanted by the server who sped by him, he found a booth and glanced at the menu.

Sterling's stomach seemed the only thing interested in the choices available. No matter how hard he tried, his head wouldn't stray far from Candy.

When the server found his table, his mind stopped wandering enough to rattle off an order for a steak and dinner salad with a regular coke—more out of habit than anything else.

As she recounted his order back to him, he looked up and nodded in agreement.

She gave him a look that screamed: *You threw a gutter ball in the tenth frame!*

Sterling had no idea if that was her actual thought, but to him, it seemed everyone had that look on their face.

Small-town mentality or his own disappointment in the current situation? He wasn't sure.

He poked around at the food on his plate and halfheartedly swallowed down what he could. His plate was about half empty when his mind snapped to attention.

He never gave up on anything. *How is this any different?*

Sure, he was only supposed to be here for a month. Sure, it was just a detour on his journey back to the pros. But dammit, he liked being around Candy.

At the very least, he deserved an answer for not returning any of his texts, and he intended to get one tonight.

Come hell or high water, Candy was going to have to talk to him.

His appetite returned, and he couldn't finish the rest of his meal fast enough. The server stopped by to check on him, and he asked for the bill.

After leaving the cash on the table along with a substantial tip, he grabbed his hat off the seat and headed for the parking lot. Candy was likely working tonight.

Sterling stopped by his motel room to grab a clean shirt—next stop, Bowling Dreams and hopefully some answers.

When he walked through the door, the place was packed. Sterling wondered if there was some special event he was unaware of or if this was just the one night all of Strawn set aside for bowling.

Candy was behind the front counter, checking in patrons and doling out bowling shoes as fast as she could.

The pink cowboy hat that sat perfectly on top of her full head of thick blonde hair matched her boots to a T. Her low-slung, hip-hugging jeans seemed molded to every one of her curves and sent Sterling's blood racing through his veins like a Thoroughbred.

When she turned and bent over to grab another pair of bowling shoes, the lights danced off the rhinestones that decorated her back pockets—as if she needed anything else to make her perfect ass look even better.

Sterling could feel his pulse immediately switch from his chest to directly behind his button-fly jeans. *Down, boy! We came here for answers, remember? And she ain't exactly interested in you right now anyway.*

Watching her interact with all her customers, he saw her personality shining like a lighthouse beacon.

Even though the music was too loud to make out what she was saying, he imagined the welcoming melody of her voice. It excited him every time they'd gotten on the phone and made him miss her more now that she'd stopped talking to him.

Candy had her back turned as he walked up to the counter. She was busy putting shoes back in their spots after hitting them with a quick spray of disinfectant.

"Seems pretty busy tonight." Sterling raised his voice over the music.

"Yup, packed. Put your name on the list there on the counter. 'Bout a twenty-minute wait," Candy replied without turning around.

"I was kinda hopin' I might catch you on a break sometime soon."

Candy finished replacing the last of her shoes and turned to face him. Her eyes widened briefly before her face lost all trace of emotion. "Now is not a good time, Sterling."

"Then when is a good time?"

"Not now, that's for dang sure. You see this place?" She motioned to the crowd behind him.

"Hey, now, I didn't come here intendin' on rufflin' your feathers." Sterling leaned both hands on the counter. "But I believe we have some talkin' to do."

"And you felt now was a good time for that?"

"I asked if you had a break comin' up, and you ain't exactly replyin' to any of my texts." He locked his eyes on hers. "So yeah, now's as good a time as any."

Candy shifted her weight from one foot to the other and shoved her hands in her back pockets. "You ain't gonna give up, are ya?"

"Ain't found a reason why I should." He bent and leaned his elbows on the counter. "You gonna give me one? Or just keep pretendin' I don't exist?"

"Ouch, cowboy."

Sterling raised his eyebrows, never looking away from Candy.

"Fine. We close at midnight." She sighed. "Come back about five minutes early, and we'll talk while I'm closin' up."

Sterling straightened and wrapped his knuckles on the counter. "See you at five till midnight."

Chapter Eighteen

CANDY SHOOK with irritation as she watched Sterling walk away from the counter and out the front door.

She'd deal with his fine ass later. Lord knew she was bowed up something fierce, and by the looks of it, he was, too.

Cracking her knuckles, she adjusted her cowboy hat and tended to the next customer. At least the alley was loud and packed with customers bowling, so no one heard their conversation.

She'd just tell him later that she didn't want to see him anymore and that it wasn't a good idea for her to be getting involved with anyone right now.

She was busy.

Trying to get her life back on track.

Who was she tryin' to convince, herself or him? Ugh. Candy shook her head and shoved Sterling from her mind.

The night went by faster than she wanted. She eyed her watch more times than she could count the last hour.

Any minute now, he was gonna walk through that door, and she'd have to face him.

Candy walked down the stretch of the lanes, making sure the servers had cleared all the beer bottles and empty coke cups. She stepped into the ladies' room and made sure all was cleaned up in there.

She stopped, eyed herself in the mirror and then wet a paper towel and wiped her face with it.

Butterflies rose in her stomach, and she snorted at the picture of how Sterling looked standing at her counter, all bound and determined to talk to her.

Long, strong legs sheathed in dark jeans and a plain white T-shirt. He'd looked beautiful.

The man floored her. She'd known him two weeks and had sex with him twice. And in the process had *completely* fallen head over heels in *like* with him.

Maybe a little *more* than like, though she'd never admit it to anyone, let alone him.

But she could admit it to herself. It didn't change anything, though. She still needed to break it off, even if the idea bugged her more than she was willing to give attention to.

No more stalling. "Put your big girl panties on and go handle this mess you got yourself into," she said to her reflection, adjusting the hat on her head.

When she stepped out of the bathroom, Sterling stood at the front counter talking to Trudie. She hadn't had much time to settle her issue with Trudie either.

May as well kill two birds with one stone. Candy took a deep breath, shook her hands out, and headed in their direction.

Sterling eyed her over the top of Trudie's bleached blonde head, and Trudie glanced over her shoulder as she approached.

"Hey, y'all." Candy made her way around the counter.

Sterling hadn't taken his eyes off her from the moment he'd spotted her. His gaze danced like a fire along her skin. She rubbed her arms and looked up at him.

"Well, I'll leave you two to it." Trudie tapped the counter with her fingernail. "Candy, why don't you give me a call tomorrow, okay?"

"Don't you want to stick around and hear this, too?" Candy crossed her arms under her chest.

"No, sugar. I don't think that's a good idea. I can tell you're still angry at me, and I understand. You just call me tomorrow, and we'll talk then." Trudie stepped away from the counter. "Night, y'all."

"Good night, Miss Trudie," Sterling said.

Candy let out a deep sigh. "Say your piece."

WITH A FROWN, Sterling crossed his arms and braced himself for the oncoming *discussion*. "And hello to you, too."

"You said we needed to talk. Talk, Sterling."

"Fine. Civility aside, I think you owe me an explanation."

Candy sighed and rested her hip against the side of the counter. "An explanation for what? We had a good time. You have work to do. I have work to do. Life moves on."

"And I have no say in this decision of yours?" Sterling tilted his head to one side, waiting for her reply.

"I didn't realize I needed to clear things through you."

"Now you're just bein' stubborn."

"Cowboy, you ain't even seen the beginnin' of stubborn."

"No offense, Candy, but that ain't right, and you know it." He rested his hands on his hips. "What the hell are you scared of?"

"Who said I was scared?"

"Okay, fine. You want to take this trip to the dentist. We'll just have to go there then."

"What the heck are you talkin' 'bout?"

"It's like pullin' teeth to get you to talk right now." He removed his hat and set it on the counter. "We meet. We have a great time. We start gettin' to know each other. Hell, we even start liking each other. Then…nothing?"

"Yeah, okay. Maybe you're right. We did have a pretty good time, but you're leavin' anyway. So what does it matter to you? It ends now, or it ends later. Either way, it ends, right?"

"See? You're scared."

"Of what? You're not makin' any sense, cowboy." She shifted her hat and ran her fingers through her hair. "I gotta finish closin' up."

"Oh, hell no, we ain't done yet. You're scared that this may actually turn into somethin'."

"What could *this* turn into? Huh? You're leavin', remember?"

"I'm goin' to play in a pro tournament. I'm not leavin' the damn country."

"Ain't no guarantee you're comin' back neither. And I'm the one who has to live in this little ass town and deal with all the rumors and talkin'." She sighed and crossed her arms. "All over again."

"That's it, isn't it?" Sterling softened his tone. "It's because of your ex."

"Don't bring him into this." She dropped her arms and straightened.

"I'm not tryin' to be mean, honey. But it makes a lot of sense."

"Fine. You got any idea how hard it is to have everyone talkin' behind your back? Everywhere you go, the looks? The pity and disgust in their eyes?" Candy looked down at her boots and wrapped her arms around her middle.

"Actually, yeah, I do." Sterling walked behind the counter and lifted her chin to gaze into her eyes. "All the talent I *threw away*. Such a promising career. Look at that drunk fool. I think I know exactly what you're talkin' about."

Candy's brows crinkled together, and she shrugged her shoulders. "Told ya I'm ruined."

Sterling ran his hand behind her neck and gently pulled her into an embrace. "Enough with the ruined already. I didn't ask you to marry me. I didn't ask you to change a thing about you. Hell, I didn't even come to this little town to do anything except prepare for Fort Worth." He rubbed her back while holding her in his arms. "But I ain't willin' to just walk away without a word."

"I didn't know what to say." She wrapped her arms around his waist. "I was just so mad."

"I want to take you out to dinner. Can we do that?"

She squeezed him tighter. "What is it with you and dinner?"

"Small town or not, you *are* entitled to a life. And goin' to dinner doesn't make you the whore of Babylon." He removed her hat and kissed the top of her head. "It makes you human."

"I'm not sure I'm ready for dinner just yet. I'm sorry."

"Then let's just get out of town. Anything. But no more silence, okay?"

"Okay." She sighed. "But I really do need to close up now."

Sterling touched his lips to hers. The soft kiss grew into a deeper one, and she responded by pressing her body tighter to his.

After breaking the kiss, he stared down at her. "Text me tomorrow?"

"Yes. Right after I wake up."

He kissed her again before grabbing his hat off the counter. "I look forward to it. Be careful gettin' home, honey."

Candy walked him to the door, and he watched as she locked it behind him.

Chapter Nineteen

CANDY HAD one heck of a time getting to sleep that night and then tossed and turned for most of it.

Sterling wanted to take her to dinner, as in a date, and she'd tried for all it was worth to figure out a reason why she shouldn't go. Every time her mind ran in a circle, the only excuse she'd landed on was the rumor mill in Strawn.

Fine, she'd just have him take her out of town.

Breckenridge, Texas, was about forty minutes outside Strawn and big enough that no one would know her there.

She grabbed her phone off her night table and sent Sterling a text. She was giving in, but she was doing it on her terms.

Feeling pretty dang proud of herself, she got up and headed for the shower. Time to get the day moving.

As Candy wrapped her wet head in a towel, she heard a knock at the front door. Wondering who it could be, she pulled her robe from the hook behind the bathroom door and went out to answer it.

After looking through the peephole, Candy sighed and opened the door.

Trudie smiled. "Hey, sugar."

"Hey there, Trudie." Candy stepped back. "Come on in."

"I figured I should just come on over and get things settled between us. I brought donuts, too." Trudie moved past her, the scent of fresh baked goods coating the air.

"Tryin' to butter me up?"

"Guilty." Trudie set the box down on the table. "G'on, get yourself finished. I'll put some coffee on."

Candy opened the box of sugary yumminess and groaned. "I tell you what, my ass sure don't need any of these but my tummy insists on me having one or…maybe three."

"Don't be silly, one or three ain't gonna kill ya. Now, scoot and get yourself done up."

"Yes, ma'am." Candy stepped from the kitchen but turned back and peeked around the corner. "You know, you look like a donut with sprinkles on it today. How many colors are you wearin' exactly? And that green satin flower you got in your hair is almost bigger than your head. Are those yellow sequins?"

Trudie guffawed. "I love it. We can count the colors and check my sequins later."

Candy laughed and returned to the bathroom to finish getting ready. When she returned to the kitchen, Trudie had the coffee done and several donuts displayed on a plate in the center of her table.

"You do not play fair." Candy grabbed a coffee mug and poured herself a cup of fresh brew.

"Sweetness, all's fair in love and friendship."

Candy sat at the table, picked a frosted chocolate donut, and took a bite. "I think that's war, not friendship." She chewed.

"Am I forgiven?" Trudie sat down and sipped her coffee.

"Only if you eat just as many donuts as me."

"Does it count that I already had two on the way here?" Trudie patted her tummy.

Candy almost choked on the bite of donut she'd just taken.

"Aw, sugar. You know I didn't mean it." She rubbed Candy's arm. "Can you forgive me?"

"I guess. I just wish you'd kept quiet. You know I had enough trouble with the cacklin' ladies over Jared and all his bull honky." Candy set her donut down. "I know it's silly, worryin' over it still. It tore me up knowin' everyone whispered behind my back each time he'd done got his dumb self in trouble. 'She should learn how to control her man.' Or, 'Why on earth doesn't she throw his hind end out?' I was a gullible fool. I let him treat me like trash, and I put up with his nastiness, but it hurt a lot knowing people had nuthin' better to do but gossip about it."

Trudie slapped her hand down on the table. "T'hell with those ol' cacklin' ladies! When it was time to be done with him, you were. And look at you now—an independent Texas woman. I'm damn proud of you, and you should be proud of yourself." A devilish smile arched her lips. "And so ya know, I've punished Billy good and fierce. No blow jobs for him for a whole week!"

"Ugh, gross! Trudie, I'm eatin' here, and I do not want to hear about you giving Billy—" She paused and shivered. "—Blow jobs."

"There's my girl. I knew that one would get ya. Aw, sweetness, c'mere." Trudie leaned over and tugged Candy into an embrace. "You gotta let that old stuff go, darlin'."

"I reckon I do. Sorry I got so mad." Candy patted Trudie's back.

"It's okay. You know I love ya, sweetheart."

"I love you, too. Now eat a stupid donut with me."

"You got it." Trudie grabbed a powdered one and took a bite.

STERLING PULLED his F-150 onto the highway, heading back toward Strawn.

He placed his hand on Candy's thigh. "Had you ever been to that restaurant before?"

"No, just billboards I passed the few times I've ever gotten a chance to get outta town." She shifted on the bench seat to sit closer to Sterling. "Cracked me up how they had so many crazy pictures all over the walls."

"I know." He chuckled. "Gotta be a good place if they have a velvet Elvis on the wall."

"And what was with our server's sideburns?" She entangled her fingers with his. "He looked like he stepped right out of a fifties movie."

Sterling checked his mirrors and changed lanes. There were few cars on the road due to the late hour, and he was grateful. He could pay more attention to the beautiful woman beside him instead of complaining about traffic.

During their meal, he'd often found himself dumbstruck and unable to speak. Completely captivated by Candy agreeing to go to dinner with him, it was everything he could do not to stare in awe when he picked her up at her trailer.

She wore a dress fitted perfectly to her hourglass shape, and her hair framed her face with thick curls. *All this and a personality to go with it*— Man, she was a one-of-a-kind.

"All he really needed was a pack of Lucky Strikes rolled up in his shirtsleeve." He glanced over to see Candy smile. "Maybe a leather jacket, too."

"Right? And that Marilyn Monroe look-alike was sumpthin else." Candy pulled one foot under her thigh.

They had about a forty-minute drive back to Strawn, and Sterling couldn't be happier about it. Driving wasn't exactly his favorite pastime, but with Candy right next to him, the time disappeared.

Their conversation was light and playful, flirting and joking the whole time. Not once did it feel forced or awkward. Even the times they sat in silence, he was happy and comfortable.

After a quiet couple of miles, Sterling moved his hand from under hers, slid it back under palm up, and threaded their fingers together. "You know? This was technically our first date."

"Is that what this was? And here this whole time, I thought we were just hungry."

"Ha-ha." He glanced over to her. "I'm serious. I think it's kinda cool. Especially since you turned me down so many times."

"Well, cowboy, if this was our first date, how come I didn't get flowers? Huh?" She bumped her shoulder into his.

"Baby, 'cause nothing could compare to how beautiful you are tonight. I didn't want the flowers feelin' outclassed."

"Oh…wowwww. Nice line." She pinched his arm. "Been savin' that one up? Or you just use that on all the girls?"

"Nah, came up with that one just for you, sweetness." Sterling flipped on the turn signal as he approached their exit.

"Well, don't I feel special?" She placed her hand over her heart to emphasize her playful sarcasm.

"Okay, okay. I'll work on some better ones for next time."

"Lines like that, and you think you're gettin' a next time? Pretty sure of yourself, ain't ya?"

"Confidence goes a long way, baby." Sterling winked at her and pulled his truck down the gravel drive to park behind Candy's. He released his seat belt, angled out, walked around the front end, and opened the passenger door for her.

Sterling took her hand. Candy stood and then thanked him.

"Walk you to your door?"

"Aren't you the gentleman?" She kept ahold of his hand. "Why, yes. I'd like that."

Sterling closed the passenger door behind her after she stepped to the side. Walking hand in hand to her front door, he felt like he was floating more than taking actual steps.

"I'd ask you in, but I'm not sure it would be appropriate." Candy bit her bottom lip.

"A cup of coffee with a beautiful woman would be nice right about now."

"Ah-ah-ah...not on a first date. I'm not that kind of girl."

"Never!" He gasped, playing along in her game. "I'd never think such a scandalous thing."

Sterling pulled her into an embrace, and she started giggling. He wrapped his arms around her tiny waist, and Candy put both hands on his chest, pretending to stop him.

"No coffee for you tonight." She rose on her tiptoes and touched her lips to his.

"I wouldn't think of offending you in such a way." He pulled her tighter to his chest, and she wrapped her arms around his neck. Sterling kissed her, tasting her as she opened for him.

When their lips parted, Candy closed her eyes and let out a breath. "Thank you, Sterling."

"You're welcome, baby. But for what?" He pulled his head back slightly to look into her eyes as she opened them again.

"For dinner. For our date. For everything." Her cheeks flushed pink, and her lips arched into a sweet smile. "I had an amazin' time, cowboy."

"Then I am a happy man." Sterling kissed her gently. "But I better get goin' before I try to violate your first date rule."

Candy wrapped her arms around his waist as she settled back down from her tiptoes. "Call me tomorrow? Maybe we can do somethin'."

"Absolutely."

With a nod, she turned to walk up the steps.

Sterling watched her unlock and open her front door and then drank in the vision of her framed by the light cast from her trailer. "G'night, Candy."

As he backed out of her driveway, Candy stayed in her doorway, watching him till he pulled out on the road. *Wild horses couldn't keep me away from that woman.*

Chapter Twenty

CANDY HURRIED out the door to pay Sterling a surprise visit.

She'd come real far in the past few days, deciding to open herself up and enjoy her time with him. She was rather proud of herself, actually.

That dinner with him had turned out better than she'd thought it would. Not that she'd thought it would be bad, especially since every time she'd been with him, he'd made her laugh, and they'd had a great time.

She parked in front of his single-story motel and stopped by the office to get his room number.

Nice thing about small towns? She knew the kid working the desk; he gave up Sterling's room number, no questions asked.

Candy walked down the sidewalk past the twenty rooms until she arrived at his door.

She stood there a moment, adjusting the straps on her pale green tank top. As she was about to knock, a case of the nerves hit, and butterflies flitted around in her stomach.

Why in the heck was she nervous? She wiped her hands on her jeans, mustered up her courage, and knocked on the door.

She heard some rustling inside and waited.

The door swung wide, and a bare chest and a pair of jeans greeted her.

"Wow! Ain't you a nice surprise to see."

Her gaze roamed up his torso to his face and then his cornflower-blue eyes. My Lord, he was a sight. Heat spread along her chest and up her neck.

The urge to lick every inch of his skin had a whole new set of butterflies swarming in her tummy. "Wow, yourself."

"Come on in." Sterling stepped to the side, allowing her room to pass him. "'Scuse the mess, I wasn't expectin' company."

"Don't fret over any'a that." Candy couldn't care less what his room looked like; she was still focused on how good he looked. Candy licked her lips. "You look...nice."

"You're lookin' at me like I'm a meal." He hooked his finger in her belt loop and pulled her close. "I kinda like it."

She rose on tiptoes and kissed him, but before things got too hot and heavy, she pulled back. With a sigh, she smiled. "You got any plans today, cowboy?"

"No, ma'am. I'm all yours."

"Would you like to accompany me to the Livestock and Craft Fair that's in town for the weekend?" Her prior feelings about being seen in public with him felt like a distant memory to her.

Now she wanted to go out with him and let the whole world see. To hell with the gossips of the town; they could all go bowl there for all she cared.

Candy wanted to have fun. And Sterling was the one she wanted to have it with.

He nodded and rested his hands on her hips. "It'd be an honor to accompany you, darlin'."

She ran her hands down his smooth-as-silk chest. "As much as I hate to say it, you probably oughta put a shirt on."

"Oh, damn. You sure about that? I heard that walkin'

around Livestock and Craft Fairs shirtless is a thing nowadays."

"Ya know what, I've heard that, too. I was debatin' takin' my top off but figured the gray-haired ladies wouldn't appreciate it."

"Miss Candy, your breasts are so perfect, I'd be tripping over myself. So you best save that treat for later."

"If you buy me a funnel cake, you can have anything you want later." Candy giggled and stepped back. "Light a fire under it. Time to show your New Mexico butt how the Texans do fairs. Plus, I wanna get there before all the good winter quilts are gone."

"My New Mexico butt, huh? All right, I'm on it." Sterling put on his shirt and grabbed his cowboy hat. "Lead the way."

STERLING HAD ONLY EVER BEEN to county fairs in Las Cruces, and they were nothing like the one in Strawn.

They were bigger, impersonal—full of rides and games and more of a carnival atmosphere. This was smaller, almost intimate, in comparison.

Everyone knew each other's names and acted like this was the biggest deal of the year. Hell, for all he knew, it was.

Candy was anxious to get to the area for the homemade quilts.

She grabbed his hand and dragged him from booth to booth, stopping to point out the intricate designs she liked and running her fingers over the texture of each one.

Sterling paid attention and hung on every word. He loved watching her eyes light up as she described the colors that would match her bedroom or couch.

He offered to buy one of the quilts she particularly liked, and she swatted his shoulder, making him laugh.

Candy was more than capable of taking care of herself and had no problem explaining that to Sterling in her own way.

Quilts gave way to hobbies. They walked through rows of everything from stained glass window hangings to miniature town models that needed a magnifying glass to see the details.

As they reached the livestock area, Sterling commented on several prized hogs and cattle.

He made good on his promise to buy Candy her funnel cake while he chose Indian fry bread. Delicious, deep-fried bread batter smothered in honey and powdered sugar, which threatened to drip on his clothes as they walked and ate.

The mechanical bull ride stopped him short, and he stared as half a dozen people stood in line to give it their best shot.

"What in the world are you thinkin', cowboy?" Candy raised an eyebrow.

"Nothin' foolish if that's what you're guessin'." He took another bite of his fry bread.

"Then what? Come on, I wanna know." She looped her arm in the crook of his elbow and leaned into his body.

"Honestly?" He glanced down into Candy's eyes and then back to the bull. "I was thinkin' about Fort Worth and how I'm gonna prove I still got it."

"You bet your ass you are." She nodded. "I have no doubt."

Sterling's heart leaped at Candy's faith in him. He tilted his head to the side as he gazed at her. "You're pretty sure, ain't ya?"

"You have to ask?" Candy pulled his arm tighter to her body.

"Nope, I guess not." Sterling kissed her. When he pulled back, he worried for a moment that she would be upset about his blatant public affection. When she didn't frown or scold him, he released the breath he'd been holding.

Sterling looked at his food and tossed the remainder of it in a nearby trash can.

"This stuff is good an' all, but I'm up for some real dinner. How 'bout you?"

"Yeah, I think you're right. Let's get outta here."

"You got any good ideas?" Sterling took her hand as they started toward the parking lot.

"I think we should go back to my place, and I'll cook. I know you've been eatin' out a lot since you've been here. Let me do a good home-cooked meal for you."

"Hard to say no when you put it like that." He pulled her in for another quick kiss as they walked.

"You can keep that up when we get to my place." Candy bumped his shoulder with hers.

Chapter Twenty-One

CANDY SWORE there was nothing hotter than a man who wasn't afraid of household chores.

Sterling stood at her kitchen sink, washing the dishes, and she couldn't keep her eyes off him.

His ass was damn near perfect, but then again, so was just about everything else on him. Long legs, strong back, chiseled chest, and a gorgeous face.

It was enough to make parts of her body she didn't even know she had tingle and pulse with awareness. And she thought she was going to stay away from him? *Yeah, right. Nice try, girl.*

"You sure you don't want me to dry or somethin'?"

"Nope. I got this, sweetness. Why don't you pick out a movie for us?"

"A movie, huh?" She couldn't help the disappointment that rose in her belly.

Here she was, undressing him in her mind and picturing all the things she wanted to do to his body, and he wanted to watch a movie? *Men are so strange.*

"Yes, ma'am. We can cuddle on the couch." Sterling looked over his shoulder and blew her a kiss.

Candy moaned. "Anything particular you feel like watchin'?"

"Nothin' specific. You pick."

"Sterling Day, can you get any more perfect? I mean, really, you'd think you were tryin' to get inside my pants or somethin'." She tidied some mail on the counter.

"Make no mistake, Miss Candy, I quite enjoy being inside your pants. But that ain't got nothin' to do with wantin' to watch a movie with you."

Candy gaped at him a moment before shaking her head and laughing. "Well, all right then."

She sat on the couch and searched the cable channels for a movie to watch. "Ooh, *Sucker Punch* is comin' on in ten minutes."

Sterling stepped into the room, wiping his hands on a dish towel. "That's definitely a romantic comedy." He laughed.

"You said pick what I want. You got a problem with my choice, cowboy?" She stood and walked to him.

"Candy Jameson, can you get any more perfect? I mean, really, you'd think you were tryin' to get me outta my pants or somethin'." He pulled her against him.

Candy wrapped her arms around his neck. "Make no mistake, Mr. Day, I quite enjoy what you got inside your pants." She kissed him.

He groaned and pulled her tighter against him as he delved deeper into her mouth.

Sweet Lord, her clit pulsed with each stroke of his tongue over hers, and she could feel her juices begin to wet her panties. She was horny, plain and simple, and only this man would do.

He ran one hand down her back to her bottom, cupped the whole cheek in his palm, and hiked her up against him. With the other, he collared her neck gently, then ran it down her chest to one breast and massaged it.

Candy tugged at his shirt and rubbed against him,

moaning as she made contact with his erection behind his jeans and felt no shame about it.

Sterling grabbed her other butt cheek and lifted her, pulling her legs around his hips.

She dragged her mouth away from his to kiss and suck at his neck. He tasted like sunshine, and she wanted to lick every inch of him.

He walked them to the couch and sat with her straddling his lap. "You're killing me."

Candy rocked against him. "Back atcha." She ran her hands down his chest and then under his shirt.

Velvet. He felt like velvet.

"You don't stop, and we won't be watchin' any movie, darlin'." He rolled his hips beneath her.

"Can't I have both?" Candy nipped at his ear.

"Baby, you can have anythin' you want."

"I like the sound of that." She pulled off her tank top and cupped her breasts in her hands.

Sterling grabbed her sides, pulled her closer, and licked over the mounds of flesh above her bra cups.

She moaned and ran her fingers through his short hair, holding him to her chest before tugging at his T-shirt. She needed to feel his skin pressed against hers.

He reached behind her and unhooked her bra.

"Dang, you're smooth." She helped him out of his shirt.

They were both topless, and she smoothed her hands down his firm chest to his belt buckle.

Sterling chuckled and tugged open the top button of her jeans. "You're gonna have to get up so you can take these off."

They both stood, and Candy stood and stripped off her jeans and panties and then watched as he did the same.

His cock was hard and stood out from his body, and she dropped to her knees in front of him. "Have mercy. I need you in my mouth."

"Oh, God damn, girl." He gripped the back of her head by her hair as she took him into her mouth.

Candy swirled her tongue around the head and then gripped the shaft in her palm. Sterling muttered an oath as she swallowed the length of him into her mouth and sucked, flattening her tongue against his shaft as she stroked him with her lips.

Her channel clenched down on itself, and her clit throbbed. She needed him everywhere. Her mouth, her pussy…anywhere he wanted.

The thought was so dirty her cheeks went up in flames, but she shoved her embarrassment aside. She wanted him and knew he wanted her, so why bother being shy about it?

"Fuck, baby." He thrust his hips and kept a tight hold on her hair, controlling her movements.

It was so good. Her body responded to all of it, and she felt her juices coating the insides of her thighs. Candy moaned around his dick and looked up at him.

"No. Fuck." He drew in a breath. "Enough, oh, fuck. Enough." He jerked from her mouth and sat on the couch, then pulled her on top of him.

"Wait!" She pushed off his lap. "We need a condom."

"Hell. My wallet, back pocket of my jeans."

Candy retrieved the small foil package and tore it open. She knelt in front of him and rolled the condom down his shaft, then straddled his lap again.

She straddled his lap and then kissed him, dragging her teeth over his bottom lip when she pulled away. "I want you so bad I can barely stand it."

"Then have me, sugar." He cupped one breast and sucked the nipple into his mouth.

Candy shivered as lightning blazed a path from the hard point in his hot mouth to her cunt. She gripped his cock and positioned him at her opening, and slid down inch by inch, seating him deep inside her channel.

"You feel like heaven, Candy." He thrust, stroking nerves deep inside her.

A fire lit inside Candy's womb as she rolled her hips, dragging her clit against his groin. "Oh, God. I love your cock."

Sterling growled, gripped her ass in his hands, and bounced her up and down on his prick.

The sound of her hips slapping against his and the tight grip he had on her ass were almost enough to send her over the edge. Her orgasm was building quickly, and she panted and moaned against his neck, unable to stop the intense pleasure from spilling from her lips.

Sterling slammed her down one last time, then gripped her hips and rocked her back and forth against him.

Her clit pulsed as it dragged against his groin. "Sweet Jesus, I'm gonna come."

He slapped her ass, and she screamed, then moved faster. Sterling scooted farther down on the cushion, changing the angle of his shaft inside her core. "Come for me, baby."

Lights exploded behind Candy's eyes, and she bit down on his neck as her body seized in orgasm. Her pussy clenched and spasmed around his cock, and he growled again.

Sterling lifted her off him, withdrawing from her still-rippling cunt, and flipped her onto her knees.

She grabbed the back of the couch and raised her ass in the air for him. "Please. Oh God, Sterling. More. I need you. Now."

He drove into her in one motion, and she cried out in pleasure. He felt so fucking good, she could barely stand it. Sweat trickled down her back as he began shuttling his thick cock in and out of her.

"My God, your ass is so fine. So fucking fine." He spread her ass cheeks with each thrust and then pressed his thumb against her small, puckered opening.

Candy jolted at the unfamiliar sensation. No one had ever touched her there.

"Easy, baby, it's okay. Just feel it."

"Sterling," she mewled.

"Yeah, baby?" He dragged some of her juices from her pussy to her ass, then pressed his thumb there again, sliding it inside.

"Oh my God. Yes." She pressed back against him. The sensation of his thumb in her ass and the thickness of his prick made her cunt clench down on him again.

"Fuck, you keep doing that, I'm not gonna last, baby."

"I can't...oh God...I can't help it." She gripped the back of the couch as her body shook from the inside out.

Sterling fucked her harder. One hand on her hip in a death grip, the other on her bottom, his thumb stroking inside her ass. "That's it, baby. Fuck yes."

She reached between her legs and rubbed her clit. "Now, oh God. Now!"

Sterling pumped faster, his hips slapping against her ass, then he groaned loud and deep as his cock jerked inside her.

His climax set off another for her. The orgasm barreled through her, causing her body to go rigid as she cried out.

Sterling released his hold on her hip and collapsed against her back, panting for breath.

She couldn't see straight, let alone catch her breath. She'd never orgasmed so hard in her life. "So..." She dragged in a breath. "About that movie?"

Sterling exhaled a laugh and tickled her side. "You're serious?"

She yelped and wiggled beneath him. "Damn straight. Besides, you said I could have anythin' I want."

Chapter Twenty-Two

STERLING HURRIED to shower and get dressed. He intended to catch Candy before her shift started at the bowling alley.

The past week had been nothing short of perfect. His bowling scores were consistently better every day, and he and Candy had been getting along as beautiful as a Southwestern sunset.

The Fort Worth tournament was just around the corner, but Sterling was itching to spend more time with Candy.

If he were being honest, lately, it'd become a toss-up between his desire to go pro again and his love of being around her.

But when it came down to it, he'd promised himself to give it his best at that tournament. Come hell or high water, he would make his name known again.

"Candy here yet?" he asked Mason as he approached the main counter at the bowling alley.

"Nope, her shift hasn't started yet." Mason scribbled on his clipboard. "How's your game shapin' up?"

"Damn good, actually. Thanks." Sterling leaned against the counter. "You seen my scores?"

"Hadn't had a chance yet, but I'm hearin' good things. Lookin' forward to you makin' us proud."

"I plan on makin' my mark." He cleared his throat, waiting.

"Oh yeah…Candy. I think I saw her saunter in to see Trudie." Mason set his clipboard down and hit a few keys on the computer. "She usually does before her shift. Gotta catch up on the gossip and all."

"Of course." Sterling chuckled. "All right, thanks."

Sterling walked into the bar area and was greeted with the sight he never seemed to tire of—Candy smiling.

She sat on one of the stools at the bar, talking with Trudie, who consistently amazed him with the color choices in her hair and clothing.

Candy, however, was stunning as always. Of course, she could make a potato sack look good.

"Hello, ladies." Sterling tipped his hat.

"Well, hellooo, handsome." Trudie fanned herself. "What can I get ya, honey? Regular coke?"

"Yes, please, ma'am." Sterling turned to Candy. "How you doin', beautiful? Lookin' as amazing as ever, I see."

"Why do your one-liners never get old?" Candy swiveled in her stool to face Sterling. "I'm doin' great, cowboy. Gonna start my shift soon. How'd I get so lucky to see you already?"

"I have ulterior motives." Sterling flashed a sly grin.

"Do I need to move farther down the bar? 'Cause I can find something to do, I'm sure." Trudy set a tall glass of coke down in front of Sterling.

"That's up to Candy. I don't much mind either way."

Candy raised an eyebrow and looked at Sterling for a moment, then turned to Trudie. "Give us a second, will ya, hon?"

"Sure thang, sweetness. Holler if ya need me." Trudie went and busied herself at the other end of the bar.

"So what's up, cowboy? My shift starts in a few minutes."

"Well, it ain't so serious that you had to send Trudie away." Sterling chuckled. "But I was thinkin' about Fort Worth comin' up."

"Right around the corner, ain't it?"

"Exactly. I need to go check out the lanes, maybe throw a few balls to get the feel of the place."

"Well, sure. That sounds like a smart idea. What's that gotta do with me?"

"Come with me?"

"What?" Candy's eyes widened. "You know I have to work, and why would you want me around? I'd probably just distract you."

"That's foolish talk, and you know it. We'll go up Sunday, check the place out, and come back Monday. It'll be perfect."

"You do make a hard offer to refuse." Candy hopped off her bar stool and smoothed out her top. "Okay, let's do it."

"A weekend out of this little town'll do you good." Sterling placed a quick kiss on the top of her head. "Now go get to work before Mason has a coronary."

"You ain't kiddin'." Candy laughed. "Let me know when you want to head out."

"I'll pop back in later."

Sterling sipped his coke while watching Candy walk out of the lounge. Trudie wiped the bar top down, conveniently working her way back toward him. *Can she be any more obvious?*

"Hey, sugar. Need a refill yet?"

"Nah. Thank you, though. I think I'm gonna go forage for some food and relax a bit tonight."

"Not gonna let me in on what ya asked Candy, are ya?" Trudie snapped her chewing gum.

"No, ma'am, not my place. Points for tryin', though." Sterling tipped his hat. "Have a good night, Miss Trudie."

Chapter Twenty-Three

EARLY AS IT WAS, Sterling knocked on Candy's door and stood surprised when she opened it, dressed and ready to go. "Well, damn, honey. I figured I'd be waking you up."

"You did say to try and be ready around ten, didn't ya? I didn't say I was awake." She opened the door wider. "You want a quick cup of coffee first, or you ready to head out now?"

"If you're ready to go, let's just hit the road. We can always stop for coffee along the way."

"Sure thing. Let me grab my bag."

"Grab your ball, too. Might as well play one or two while we're there."

She glanced over her shoulder at him. "No strip bowling this time. Sorry to disappoint."

"Damn. Forget it, then. I don't wanna go." Sterling looked down and kicked a rock with the toe of his boot.

Candy laughed and then disappeared into the trailer. When she returned, she had her overnight bag *and* bowling ball. After handing him both, she turned and locked the door.

. . .

AFTER GETTING TO FORT WORTH, they stopped for lunch. The freedom of spending the day together kept them glued to each other.

Candy mentioned how she'd only been there a couple of times and how she enjoyed the feel of the bustling city in comparison to Strawn.

Sterling loved hearing her comments on the tall buildings and watching her point out sculptures and statues that grabbed her attention.

They remained consumed with each other, whether it was conversation, holding hands, a glance, or a smile.

He took his time getting them to the bowling alley where the tournament was scheduled. Hell, if he actually had to throw a ball down the lane, it'd mean he wouldn't be able to have his hands all over Candy in some way.

He finally relented and found his way to the alley at her suggestion. They played a few games, and he got a good feel for the place.

Seemed she was looking out for him, knowing what he needed to do before he could admit it to himself.

That didn't stop her from returning all the affection, though. A herd of bulls couldn't have pulled them apart.

A lot of the tournament decorations and booths were in various states of being set up. Some done already, some well on their way.

Sterling realized it'd been some time since he'd been around something of this level of importance within the bowling community.

Butterflies wrestled around in his stomach, and he tried his best to push them aside.

Candy came up behind him and wrapped her arms around his waist, silently reassuring him that he was right where he needed to be.

"Let's get checked in at the hotel I reserved. Maybe go grab some dinner." Sterling rubbed his hands over hers.

"You sure? You don't want to throw a few more?"

"Yeah, I'm sure. I got a good feel for the lanes." Sterling turned and put his arm around her shoulders. "What're you hungry for tonight?"

"You." Biting her bottom lip, she gazed up at him.

"Really now?" His mind immediately flashed to a vision of her hair spread across his stomach. "You sure that's gonna be enough for you?"

"Okay. You *and* room service. That's what I'm in the mood for." She squeezed his side a little tighter.

"Sure you don't wanna hit a restaurant or somethin'? Then back to the hotel?"

"Not for what I'm hungry for. You heard me, cowboy. You, me, food, hotel room." She pushed up to her tiptoes and nibbled on his earlobe.

"Oh, holy hell, baby. You have the best ideas." Sterling sat and unlaced his shoes, suddenly unable to remove them fast enough. "Let's get outta here."

"I have a problem, though." Candy did the same as he gathered up their gear to leave. "I can't decide if you're gonna be dessert...or the main course."

CANDY WIPED the corner of her mouth with her napkin and pushed her empty plate to the side. "What's on your mind?"

"A few things. Am I really ready for this? What's it gonna feel like to have all those people surrounding me again?" Sterling wheeled their food service cart out the door and left it in the hallway.

Candy sat on the bed and patted the space next to her. "Spill it, cowboy. Talk."

"Truth is, I'm more nervous than a new cow feeling the

heat off the branding iron. Like he knows what's coming, yet he understands it's just his time."

"Sweetie, you have worked real hard for this comeback. I don't know another man who deserves it more than you do." She kissed his cheek.

"I don't know about the deservin' part, but I have worked hard. Done the best I can, ya know?" Sterling pinched her chin between his fingertips and kissed her.

His tenderness toward Candy warmed her to her toes. Here he was, spilling his guts out, fears and all, and still managed to make her melt.

This was his time to shine. He would make his comeback, and his dream would be complete. It made her sad, though, because she knew it meant she'd probably never see him again.

"It's gonna work out. You'll see." She forced a smile. "Let's see if I can help take your mind off the stress." Candy rose from the bed and tugged off his boots, then unbuttoned her blouse, tossed it to the floor, and stepped between his legs.

"Tournament? What tournament?" He ran his hands up her sides to her breasts. "I think I need some of my Candy."

"Yes, you do, baby." She unhooked her bra and slid the straps down her arms.

Sterling cupped her breasts in both hands and took a nipple into his lips.

She moaned as the heat of his mouth spread over every inch of her skin. He made her body feel *too* much, and all of it had started settling in her heart.

He unbuttoned her jeans and pushed them and her panties down her legs, then removed his clothes.

Candy climbed onto the bed, and he followed. She wrapped her body around his and kissed him.

Sterling made her feel like she was tiny and petite. Like she was precious. It did more to heal her battered heart than she'd ever dreamed possible.

If she wasn't careful, she'd end up handing it over to him before this night was over. Maybe she already had.

Candy let herself go with it, throwing all worries of protecting her heart to the wind as he took his time exploring every inch of her skin and each curve of her body.

She explored him, too, reveling in the hard planes of his chest, the tight ridges of his abs.

Sterling rolled Candy to her back and donned a condom before settling between her thighs.

Raising her knees high on his hips, she linked her ankles at his lower back, holding him tight against her body.

Every inch of their flesh touched, sending ripples of tingling sensations through her. She raised her head and sucked at the tender skin of his neck.

Sterling drew in a shuddering breath when she nipped the edge of his ear and then ran his large, calloused hands up her arms, raising them above her head.

Candy arched against him, causing the hard points of her nipples and full breasts to slide against his bare, muscled chest.

She looked up at him, and he pressed his forehead to hers, meeting her gaze as he entered her swollen sex with deliberate, measured thrusts.

Candy moaned as her willing flesh gave way, accepting his swollen crown and thick shaft.

Seating himself fully within her channel, he closed his eyes, panting, and then kissed her.

Candy sought his tongue and sucked it into her mouth, and he rolled his hips, moving inside her.

This was far different from the sex they'd had before.

Slow passion; careful, intense touches. It felt a lot like making love, and she got caught in the undertow and dragged under willingly.

Candy let herself be swept away in the current of power, holding her captive, named Sterling Day.

. . .

CANDY WOKE in the cocoon of Sterling's arms. She glanced at the clock on the nightstand and cringed. It was already past ten. They needed to get moving and check out of the room.

Careful not to wake him, she moved from his arms and tiptoed into the bathroom. She needed a little time to sort out her feelings, and the shower was the perfect place to do that.

Last night, she'd made a choice to push away her fears while trying to soothe his.

Did he know she was starting to have feelings for him? Not likely, and it would probably be better in the long run if he didn't.

She didn't want to distract him from his goal; his dream of a comeback was a priority for him. And she wanted that for him.

One more week. Candy had one more week to enjoy her bowling cowboy, and then he'd be gone.

And then, she'd let him go because that's what he would need her to do.

Chapter Twenty-Four

HEADING out to Fort Worth was the second smartest thing Sterling had done since he got to Strawn.

Finding Candy was most definitely the first.

She supported his desire to succeed and had him smiling every time he so much as caught a glimpse of her.

He stepped up his practice schedule as the tournament loomed closer, careful not to leave out his physical therapy for his shoulder.

Yet every evening, he made a point of seeing Candy before her shift started, and he wished her a good night.

Somewhere in the last few weeks, the importance of turning pro again took a backseat to wanting to make Candy proud of him.

Focus wasn't the problem. He stayed determined to win, but this little small-town girl made an impact on him.

As his departure date closed in on him, he found Candy on his mind more often than not. *Knock it off. Tournament, remember?*

Thursday night, he decided to surprise Candy with food for her lunch break.

He pushed through the entry doors with his shoulder as he

balanced a drink carrier in one hand and a bag of sub sandwiches in the other.

Setting his haul on the rental counter, he scanned the alley for her and waited.

Candy walked out from the door on the far side of the building, leading to the pinsetting machines behind the lanes.

Her eyes sparkled as she walked toward Sterling at the front counter, and her full lips spread into a smile. "Well, ain't this a sweet surprise. What are you doin' here so late?"

"I thought you might appreciate something different than bar food tonight." Sterling held up the bag. "I hope you like subs."

"That sounds perfect." She beamed. "I can only eat deep-fried everything for so long."

"Besides, it's a good excuse to see you before I head off to bed."

"I don't remember you ever needin' an excuse before." She leaned up on her tiptoes to kiss him on the cheek. "Thank you."

Even a quick kiss from Candy sent his heart racing. "Lead the way, beautiful." Sterling grabbed the food and drinks off the counter.

He followed her back to the office and pulled the sandwiches out of the bag as she cleared space on the desk for them to eat.

"How are you feelin' about this weekend?" Candy pulled a straw from its paper wrapper and placed it in one of the coke cups.

"Better than I have in years." He handed her one of the sandwiches and then unwrapped his. "Plannin' on headin' out Saturday morning nice and early."

"I was wonderin' what the plan was. I'm really excited for you." She removed the paper from her sandwich and took a bite. "What are you gonna do for your last day in Strawn?"

"Funny you ask. I was hopin' this hot little cowgirl I met might be up for some company tomorrow night."

"Hot little cowgirl, huh? Do I know her?"

"You might. Sexy little number, 'bout yay high." He motioned with his hand. "Full of spit and vinegar."

"Drawin' a blank. And this *is* a small town." She sipped her coke. "Might have to give me a better description."

Sterling chuckled, almost choking on his sandwich. "Oh, I'm sure you've seen her around." He took a quick sip of his coke to clear his throat. "Think you might be interested in seein' me before I leave?"

"Aw, honey, you know I have to work tomorrow night."

"I know. How 'bout I meet you here a bit before you close the place up?" Sterling took another bite.

"I got a better idea. Meet me at my house after I'm off." She nudged him under the table with her foot. "We can watch a movie together."

"Deal. And baby, we can do anything you want." Sterling finished the last of his sandwich.

"I'm glad you decided to visit me tonight." Candy wrapped up the remaining portion of her sandwich. "I'm sorry, but I gotta get back to it now."

"So soon?" He picked up the trash from their meal and tossed it in the nearby wastebasket.

"Yeah, I rarely take a full-blown lunch break. But I'm happy I did tonight."

"Perfect. Me, too." Sterling stood as she walked around to his side of the desk. He pulled her body in close to his and kissed her. "Then you should probably stop slackin' and get back to work."

"Tomorrow night, then?"

"Absolutely, I can't wait."

Candy moved things back into their place on Mason's desk and then returned to Sterling's arms. Her head was at the perfect height to lean against his chest. "Let's plan on that then."

"I'll see you soon." Sterling kissed the top of her head. "Have a great night, baby."

They walked out of the office, and Sterling headed for the exit.

On his way out the doors, he looked back over his shoulder with mixed emotions and watched her as she walked behind her counter.

Excited to have Fort Worth finally on his doorstep, yet sad that his amazing month with Candy was at an end. Really, though, it could have been six months, even a year. Still too short. Still not enough.

How was he going to do this without his Candy?

My Candy?

Chapter Twenty-Five

CANDY PULLED into her gravel driveway next to her trailer with an ache in her chest.

Sterling wasn't there yet, which was good because it'd give her a little time to freshen up and get her head on straight.

She'd thought about him constantly in the last week. Things had changed for her during that little overnight trip she'd taken with him to Fort Worth.

Her heart had double-crossed her mind, and now she was stuck. She'd fallen head over heels for him.

Sterling was leaving tomorrow morning, and even though her belly burned in disappointment at the prospect of never seeing him again, she knew it was for the best.

Candy took a deep breath and rubbed the spot on her chest that kept up its ache. *Suck it up, girl. You can do this.*

Stepping into her trailer, she left the door unlocked for him and headed for the bathroom. She pulled her hair in a high ponytail, took off her makeup, and donned a pair of comfy pants and a T-shirt.

Candy headed back out to the kitchen to make a fresh pot of coffee and found Sterling leaning against the counter with a single red rose in his hand and the coffee already brewing.

"Hey. Whatcha got there?"

"Just a little somethin' I thought you might like."

"My heart." She pressed her hand to her chest. "That's so sweet."

Candy couldn't remember the last time anyone had brought her flowers. They had joked about it on their date, but she hadn't paid it much mind.

Now, here she was, feeling all giddy and like a schoolgirl because he'd thought enough to bring her a rose.

"Not sweeter than you. And to be honest, I can't tell if you look better in those little outfits you love to wear or how you look right now." He pulled her into his arms.

Her cheeks tingled as a blush crept up her neck to her face. "Sterling Day, have you lost your marbles?"

"Not a chance." Setting the rose down, he kissed her. "I know beauty when I see it, and you, Candy Jameson, have it in spades."

The heat that had taken over her cheeks spread down through her body, and she wrapped her arms around his neck.

Why did he say these things to her? It only made her want him more. And that couldn't happen. *Dammit.*

Smoothing her hand up the back of his neck, she pulled him down for another kiss.

He sucked her bottom lip and then gently nibbled it. Moaning, she melted against him as longing replaced the warmth. How could she let him go?

Pulling away, he gazed down at her. "You okay, sweetheart?"

She couldn't speak for fear that all the thoughts rolling around her mind might come tumbling out. She nodded instead.

"All right then." He kissed her forehead. "Coffee's ready." Stepping aside, he motioned to the counter. "I brought something else."

Hiding behind him were two grocery bags. "Ooh, what's

that?" Candy opened the sacks. "Ice cream? Oh, my word, and chocolate syrup, too?"

"Yes, ma'am. Let's not forget this." Sterling pulled out a can of whipped cream. "I can think of lots of fun things to do with this." Popping the cap, he tilted his head back and squirted a generous amount into his mouth.

"Sterling Day, what on earth?"

"C'mere, baby," he said with a mouthful of cream.

Candy giggled as he took her into his arms and kissed her.

All that sweet, fluffy cream flowed between their lips as they stroked their tongues together.

Images passed through her mind of licking the sweet treat off his body, and her nipples hardened at the thought.

"Mmm." She broke the kiss and cocked one brow. "Fun indeed."

Gazing down at her, Sterling grinned. "Candy Jameson, did you just have a dirty thought?"

"Not me. Nope. Never." She widened her eyes and cleared her throat.

"Well, damn. I'd kinda like it if you did." Stepping away, he pulled two bowls from a cabinet and set them on the counter.

"I bet you would." Bumping his hip with her own, she grabbed two spoons from the drawer, and Sterling found her ice cream scoop in the other drawer.

He chuckled and popped the lid off the ice cream, scooping a generous amount into each bowl. "Just sayin'."

Candy sat back and watched in awe as he topped both with the chocolate syrup and then the whipped cream.

This amazing man had carved out a little place inside her home…and her heart.

Sometime in the last month, he'd become so familiar to her—and with her—that she couldn't imagine not having him here.t

What the heck was she going to do? The ache returned in full force, and she rubbed her chest.

"Hand me the jar of cherries, sweetheart?" Sterling turned and put the container of ice cream in her freezer.

Swallowing past the lump that had formed in her throat, Candy fished the jar from the bag and set it next to the bowls.

Her eyes burned, and she blinked, trying to force back the tears that had started to form. *Crap. Crap. Crap.*

"Thanks, honey." Opening the jar, Sterling glanced at her. "How many do you—hey, what's wrong? You look like somebody just kicked your puppy." He reached for her, but she shrugged and picked up the forgotten rose.

"I'm fine. Everything's perfect." *Except you're leaving.* She pressed the petals to her nose and drew in a breath. "I need to put this pretty thing in water." Grabbing a bud vase from the cabinet, she filled it with water. "I love roses. Thank you."

"You're welcome, baby." He kissed her cheek. "Why don't you go pick a movie? I'll pour us some coffee and bring our treats into the living room."

After finishing their sundaes, Candy laid her head in Sterling's lap. He pulled her hair free from the tie, ran his fingers through it and played with the ends for near the whole rest of the movie.

She didn't pay much attention to the TV, though. How could she? This was it. Her last night with him.

It was just about a month ago she'd told herself she'd just enjoy him and have fun, then when it was time for him to go, she'd send him off with a sweet kiss and a good luck wish.

She turned on her back and gazed up at him. How could she let him go now?

He stroked his fingers through her hair once more.

Candy let out a soft sigh. "You ready for bed?"

"I am." He traced her nose with his fingertip.

She sat up and faced him. "Take me to bed, please?"

"Candy, I—"

"Shh." She placed her finger against his lips. "Don't. Just take me to bed and make love to me."

He stood, took her hand, and led her to her bedroom. She didn't want to talk about it. Didn't want to waste their last night talking about what she was feeling.

She wanted to have these last hours and just feel him.

GOD ABOVE, *this woman is amazing.* Sterling caressed her silky skin and full curves as he let his senses drink in every ounce of her.

Even as they lay together in the dim light filtering in through her bedroom blinds, the image of her beautiful body stayed imprinted in his mind.

His hands and lips were more than eager to clarify any parts that remained hazy.

He paused long enough to retrieve a condom from his pants pocket. Tearing open the foil package, he rolled it on his erection and climbed back into bed.

He balanced himself on one elbow as he let his other hand trail from the edge of her jaw, down her throat to her collarbone.

Dipping his head, he pressed his mouth to the side of her neck, taking his time as he placed kiss after kiss down the top of her breast.

She arched into him, moaning, when he closed his lips around her tight, budded nipple.

Everything about this woman drew him in. The sexual attraction was obvious from the moment they met, but what was between them had become something more.

As they lay skin-to-skin in the dark of her bedroom, he found he wanted to know even more about her.

She shifted her body under him, her full breasts pressing against his chest, and pulled him between her inviting thighs.

Wrapping her arms around his back, she scored him with her nails, then moved down his spine to his ass as she adjusted her hips and spread her legs farther to receive him.

Candy reached between them then, fisting her small hand around his shaft.

With a growl, Sterling tangled his fingers in her hair and bit down on her shoulder.

He thrust his hips forward, sliding within her grip, as white-hot heat snaked up his spine. "Fuck, your hand feels amazing."

"I want you inside me." She bit his bottom lip and stroked him again, and his prick throbbed, growing thicker in response.

Sterling pulled her hand away and slipped inside her sweet channel, shuddering when her tight heat encased his length.

The struggles and hard-fought battles had brought him to this place in time; all else seemed minor in comparison.

He had found a little piece of heaven within this moment.

"Sterling," she whispered against his mouth.

They moved in perfect unison as their lips met. Bodies pressed together, slick with sweat and lust.

No fighting for control, no walls to scale; this was a fire, a passionate, sensual cauldron melting down two and creating one.

The heat of it scalded him to the bone.

His breathing grew heavy, and he slowed his movements, desperate to gain some measure of control in the presence of his building climax.

The little moans and gasps escaping Candy grew louder as she pulled him closer, shifting her hips to take him deeper and grinding her clit against his groin.

Sweet God. As his pace quickened, the grip of her tight cunt and the sting of her nails in his back shared how close she was as well.

She bit his shoulder hard, and his control shattered.

They climaxed together, their moans dancing in the air around them before she dragged her teeth from his shoulder and took his mouth in a deep, passionate kiss.

Her tongue tangled around his own with a fevered intensity he'd never experienced before. With her legs still wrapped around his waist, he trembled above her and took all she wanted to give him.

Breaking the kiss, he rolled them to the side and pulled her tight to his chest, savoring the feel of her body against his.

Neither of them said anything, and after a few minutes, Sterling got up to dispose of the condom.

Getting back in bed, he pulled the sheet over the top of them. She released a soft purr as she nuzzled into his chest, and he kissed the top of her head.

The faint smell of jasmine drifted up from her thick tresses as he ran his fingers through it, and it wasn't long before he felt her body relax into sleep.

His chest swelled at the sheer contentment of having her in his arms, and he drifted to sleep.

Chapter Twenty-Six

A LOW, rhythmic beeping roused him, and he forced his eyes to open, realizing it was the alarm on his cell phone. He'd set it for an early start to compensate for the drive.

Sterling reached with his free arm to silence the intrusion and knew he had to get on his way to Fort Worth for the tournament today.

He carefully untangled his arm from Candy and the sheets, not wanting to wake her. She might want to sleep in if she could.

After a quick shower, he set up the coffeepot to brew a fresh batch and searched for a pen and paper.

He penned the note, and as he signed it, he wanted to write so much more. *Get a grip, cowboy. It's time to go.*

After downing a quick cup of coffee, he walked back to Candy's bedroom, leaned over the bed, kissed her forehead, and drifted his hand over her soft, enticing curves, hoping his touch might rouse her.

No such luck, though; she just let out a soft sigh in response but didn't wake.

With a sigh, Sterling retrieved his duffle bag and headed for the door, picking up his hat on the way out.

A deep breath of the fresh morning air steeled his resolve; he had a tourney to win and a few miles to drive to get there.

Fort Worth needed to prepare because he was coming to get his championship back.

CANDY TURNED on her side as sunshine filtered through the blinds covering her bedroom window. *Sterling*.

Pulling the other pillow lying empty in the bed to her chest, she buried her nose in the soft cotton pillowcase, catching the slight lingering scent of him, and moaned.

"Sterling?" She sat up. "Sterling, you still here?"

No reply.

It was only eight in the morning, and dang if she didn't feel like she needed to sleep another six hours. She dragged her deliciously sore limbs from the warm bed in hopes she'd find him in her trailer still.

When she entered the kitchen, she kept going and looked into the living room—there were no signs of him.

So much for a sweet kiss and a good luck wish. Disappointment settled around her like a thick, wet blanket of emotion.

Brushing her hair back from her face, she scolded herself for her foolishness. She wasn't some naïve girl who thought sex meant anything more than just…sex.

So what if they'd spent the last month together?

It didn't have to mean anything.

Beyond no Sterling, the first thing she spied was a pot of coffee that'd been brewed at some point. The second was the note on the table.

She poured herself a cup of the lukewarm brew, placed it in the microwave to warm, and read the note.

CANDY,
I HAD TO LEAVE EARLY TO GET TO MY TOURNAMENT. I
DIDN'T HAVE THE HEART TO WAKE YOU.
CALL OR TEXT ME, OKAY?
WISH ME LUCK, DARLIN.
STERLING

She set the note back down in its place on the table and grabbed her coffee from the micro.

Should she text or call him? Or maybe she should just leave it be.

She debated with herself, toasted a bagel, slathered it with cream cheese, and wandered over to her living room.

Maybe they'd be broadcasting the tournament, and she'd get to watch him compete. Would've been nice if she could've gone with him, but he hadn't asked her.

Honestly, what in Sam Hill made her think he would have? Nothing, that's what.

Candy shook her head at her stupidity and bit down on her bagel. She was far smarter than this. It was, after all, just supposed to be fun and a few dates and some really good sex.

In fact, it was the best sex she'd ever had. Big deal, though; it was no relationship, that was for sure.

She'd had a good—no, a *great* time with him, and if she ever got to see him again? Well, she sure wouldn't turn him away.

A man on a mission was what Sterling was. Dead set on going pro again. He'd make it, too, and she doubted there was room for her in his agenda.

With a sigh, she clicked on the TV and searched the guide to see if the tourney would be on at some point.

Looked like the finals were scheduled to air tomorrow. It meant he'd be bowling all day, working his way through the eliminations.

She finished her small breakfast while watching the local news, then decided heading back to bed was a better idea.

After depositing her dirty dishes in the sink, Candy crawled beneath the covers. She just needed more sleep, a sure remedy for the sadness settling in her gut.

With any luck, it'd be gone by time she woke up. If not, she figured she'd clean her little home top to bottom before heading to work.

That ought to do it. Her last thought as she pulled the blankets over her head was maybe she'd text him later tonight and see how he fared.

This way, she wouldn't distract him while he competed during the day.

If she'd learned anything about bowlers all these years working at the alley, it was they were serious about keeping their focus.

With her decision made, she fell back asleep.

Chapter Twenty-Seven

Youthful vigor thrummed through Sterling stronger than it had in years.

His shoulder was loose and limber, and his goals clear as a summer sky.

And there was Candy. Every time the thought of her crossed his mind, his lips curved into a smile. *Why didn't I ask her to come with me?*

Chances were, she would have been bored anyway. She was already stuck working in a bowling alley, as it was. Why on earth would she want to spend the whole day watching him bowl?

On the one hand, he knew she enjoyed being with him, and damn if he didn't like spending every minute he could with her.

After he'd found a decent parking space, he tried his best to clear his mind as he gathered his duffle. Stepping up to the double-door entrance, he put his hand on the silver handle and pulled.

The blast of energy slammed into him and rattled his nerves before he realized the symphony of tournament play was just what he had been missing.

Layer upon layer of voices and music, the bright lights of the scoreboards, the shattering of pins—he was home.

Searching through the crowds for any sign of where he needed to go, he caught sight of the registration booth and moved his boots in its direction.

His path led him through a maze of competitors, spectators, and employees. *Lordy, this place is packed.*

He stepped to the booth and set his bag at his feet. "Howdy, ma'am, I'm here to check in." *Wonder if anyone will remember me.*

The woman, who appeared to be in her mid-fifties, looked up from her stack of papers to greet him. "Name?"

"Sterling Day, ma'am." Tipping his hat. "I prequalified in Las Cruces."

"Let me see…" She flipped through a few pages, scanning them for his name. "Here you are. We were wondering if you were going to show up. Sign-in started half an hour ago. Not much time left for warm-ups."

"Long drive." He hooked a thumb behind his large belt buckle. "I'm good, though. I got some practice in last night."

"That's good. On behalf of the tournament, we'd like to wish you the best of luck this weekend."

Sterling figured she must have the good luck wishes memorized like a charm if she had to do this all weekend. "Thank you, ma'am."

"Sterling Day…why does your name sound so familiar?" She tapped her pen against her bottom lip. "Wait, I know you. Aren't you the one who hurt his shoulder several years ago after winning the PBA championship?"

He let out a sigh. "Yes, ma'am. Long story, but I'm back now. Gonna see if I got one more in me."

"Personally, I thought it was a shame when it all happened." She offered her hand to shake. "I can't tell you how happy I am to see you back at it."

"Thank you very much, ma'am." Sterling shook her hand and was rewarded with a fine, genuine smile from the lady.

"I remember watching you back then. You had some real talent." She withdrew her hand and gave him his packet of tournament information. "Go get 'em, cowboy."

He took the manila envelope from her. "Gonna try my best."

Retrieving his bag from the floor, he stepped aside from the booth and found a nearby corner to shuffle through the contents of the packet he'd received.

He was in the first bracket, slated to start in thirty minutes.

The woman was right, not much time at all for a warm-up.

Gathering all the papers in one hand, he reached into his bag with the other and looked for a sucker. Finding it, he unwrapped it and popped it in his mouth.

Memories of his first meeting with Candy came floating by.

You throw one heck of a ball. You ever think of goin' pro?

Sterling smiled, and his heartbeat sped up with thoughts of her racing through his mind. He blew out a breath. "I better get to it then."

Grabbing his bag once more, he headed to his scheduled spot.

I knew you had too much talent for just any cowboy.

He smiled. Candy may not have been at the actual tournament, but as far as he was concerned, she was *with* him, cheering him on.

STERLING RIPPED through the first bracket of eliminations like a freight train. He'd thrown his ball down the lane better than he ever had.

He rubbed his shoulder, out of habit more than anything, and was surprised to find it didn't ache for a change.

By time Candy arrived at Bowling Dreams for her Saturday night shift, she'd pretty much tuckered herself out cleaning her whole trailer.

She'd scrubbed the bathroom so clean someone could eat in there, not like anyone would, though.

All the cleaning had been a useless attempt to scrub Sterling from her mind. It hadn't worked, and walking into Bowling Dreams only made it worse.

She glanced at lane ten, and visions of Sterling filled her mind. Good Lord, would she ever be able to look at it again and not think of him?

Just the thought of what she'd done with Sterling there the first night they'd met had equal parts longing and arousal pumping through her body. *How confusing.*

Candy stepped behind the front desk. "Hey, Mason." She breezed past him into the back office.

"Evenin'." Mason nodded.

She grabbed a fresh drawer from the safe and returned to the front desk. "Got anyone on the roster for Rock-n-Bowl tonight?" She set the drawer down next to the register.

Mason grabbed the clipboard from below the counter. "Looks like about twenty so far." He handed it to her. "Thinkin' we might just have a few more. Folks are all riled up about the tourney in Fort Worth, I'm guessin'."

She perused the list. "Dang, even the Turners are coming out tonight?"

He nodded at her and started cashing out the register so they could change shift.

"Tell you what, Mason. We're probably the strangest town in Texas. You'd think we'd be all about rodeoin' or farmin'. Nope, not the good citizens of Strawn. They bowl." She let out an unladylike snort and put her drawer in the register once he'd removed his.

"You know the story as well as anyone. Hometown Boy made it big forty years ago, and it was all uphill from there." He chuckled. "Course he came back here afterward, built this place, married my mother, and along came baby Mason Jr." He grinned and disappeared into the office, shutting the door behind him.

Candy shook her head and wondered, not for the first time, why anyone would ever come back to this place.

Then again, that was forty years ago—a different time, maybe even a different place.

She tossed a wave to Trudie when she poked her head out the service bar window, then set to preparing herself for what might well be the busiest night they'd see all year.

The place was full of energy tonight, and it helped a great deal to distract her. Candy only had time to think of Sterling a few thousand or so times, though she still hadn't texted him. *Heaven help me.*

As things started to wind down and closing time neared, she pulled her phone from her back pocket and stared at his contact info. *Too late to text him now.*

She had no idea how late the tourney went; it was probably long over by now, and the poor man was likely catching up on some much-needed sleep.

They'd been up pretty late last night.

Candy shook her head, stuffed her phone back into her pocket, and checked out another customer.

When the last bowlers were out of the building, and the servers were milling about clearing tables, she checked the time.

Dang, it's midnight. What if he was waitin' to hear from me?

She pulled out her phone and typed a message. *Fat chance, he ain't waitin' on me...*

But what if? Before she could talk herself out of it, she

sent him the text: just a simple question asking how he did and an apology for not texting sooner.

She just hoped he was sleeping and would get the message in the morning.

Chapter Twenty-Eight

"THIS IS your requested wake-up call for room six-oh-two. It is now seven a.m."

Sterling listened to the programmed voice relay its message, hung up the receiver, and tried to rub the sleep from his eyes.

Dang, morning came way too early. After a good yawn and stretch, he swung his heavy legs over the side of the bed and let his feet drop to the floor.

Staring at the clock on the nightstand, he cursed himself for staying up too late last night.

He'd had a rough time settling his mind after a phenomenal day in the brackets. All he wanted to do was share his success with Candy, but exhaustion had won after lying in bed watching TV and giving into his new obsession of checking his phone repeatedly to see if it was working.

No call.

No text message.

Eyeing his cell on the nightstand, Sterling gave in to the temptation and allowed himself to check his phone one more time before he *had* to get in the shower.

Just as a precaution, of course.

Dorothy F. Shaw & T. D. Hoffman

One SMS Message

> Candy: How did you do today? Sorry I didn't text sooner, busy night.

Well, hell, if that didn't beat all. Of course, it being Saturday night and all, she'd been busy last night. Feeling downright foolish for staying up waiting to hear from her, he typed in a quick message.

> Sterling: Going great here, so far. 2 more eliminations today before finals tonight. Wish me luck.

He hit the send button and stared at the screen for a while longer. Giving in to his desire for her, he typed one more message and hit send before he talked himself out of it.

> Sterling: Missin my favorite Candy. And I ain't talkin bout my suckers. 😊

He couldn't help himself. Smiling, he tossed his phone on the nightstand, pushed himself out of bed, and started for the bathroom.

He had a tournament to get back to.

By two o'clock Sunday afternoon, he had cemented his position in the finals and had earned the rest of the afternoon off.

The last round had run long and pushed him through lunch. Starving and grateful for the break, he stood staring at his reflection in the bathroom mirror, refreshed from the cold water he'd just run over his face.

Despite how great he had felt after yesterday, today had been a much bigger challenge, and his shoulder was hollering at him for it.

The finals were scheduled for six that night. Plenty of time to ice down his shoulder at the hotel, grab a bite to eat and maybe even a nap.

After drying his hands, he checked his phone for the umpteenth time.

Still no reply from Candy.

Sterling put the cell back in his pocket in an unsuccessful attempt to put it out of his mind. *Would've been nice to have her here for the final round.*

THE ANNOYING DING of her cell phone rang out, letting Candy know she had a message waiting.

Eyes still closed, she felt around for the phone on her night table and almost knocked the lamp over.

Gripping the device by the charging cord, she pulled it toward her face and flipped it open.

Sterling!

She bolted upright, holding the phone in her now shaking hands, and read the messa—wait, two messages?

He'd sent her two messages!

"Thank you, baby Jesus." Bouncing on the bed, she squealed when she read the part about him missing her. *That's right, you* do *miss your Candy!*

She started to type a text back to him but stopped short, realizing his message had come in over three hours ago, and he was probably neck deep in the last eliminations.

Glory, he'd made it this far; she sure as heck didn't want to distract him with any girly nonsense.

With a deep sigh, she lay back on her pillow and thought about all the different things she wanted to reply to him.

Gah, could she get any cheesier? Probably. Did she care at the moment? Heck. No.

Her cowboy had texted her back.

Whoa! Her cowboy?

That thought sobered her right quick. When in the world had he become *her* cowboy?

Candy let out an exasperated sigh and rubbed her eyes. Things had felt so perfect their last night together, and she couldn't help but wonder if they could've had some sort of future together.

The truth of it was, Sterling *was* hers now.

Candy had planned to get the heck out of this town someday. Maybe he was the one to help her do that. It seemed impossible now, though.

She turned over and prayed, staring at the window blinds, that maybe, just maybe, she'd see him again.

A loud banging on her front door jolted her from her thoughts.

Untangling herself from the blankets and the cell phone still attached to its charging cable, she got out of bed.

"Who is it?"

"It's Trudie, sugar. Open up. I brought goodies."

Candy glanced at the clock: 4:30 p.m. Dang, she'd slept all day. She swung the door wide and stepped aside, letting Trudie pass.

"Land sakes, child. Were you sleepin'?" Trudie asked as she zoomed past Candy into the kitchen, her high heels tapping on the linoleum floor.

Where this woman got her energy, Candy had no idea.

Maybe she ran on nuclear power? She sure glowed as if she did. At some point between last night's shift and now, Trudie had dyed a hot pink streak in her bleached head of hair.

Trudie was a work of art from her flowing pink tank top, fitted Capri jeans, and high-heeled slip-on shoes. Not classic art, but art just the same.

"Me? Still sleepin'? 'Course not. This is my newest

fashion statement. You like?" Candy approached the kitchen counter with a runway walk, stopped in front of the coffeepot and cocked a hip. Grabbing a mug, she filled it and then set it in the microwave to warm. "Speakin' of fashion statements, you get in a tussle with the pink panther today?"

"*You* like?" Trudie mimicked Candy's words and then fluffed her coifed head of *very* big hair.

"I do. It's very…you." Candy laughed and retrieved her cup, sipping the now-hot brew.

"Billy loves it. Says it makes him feel like he's got a new woman in his bed every time I change it." Trudie wagged her brows.

"Hello? TMI! I do *not* want to think about you and Billy Masters in bed together. I'm fresh outta brain bleach."

"Never mind that now." Trudie held up the bottle of tequila and a bag of tortilla chips. "The tourney is on in a coupla hours. I reckon we can have a girls' evenin' and watch together."

"Do I have a choice?" Candy peered at her friend over the rim of her mug.

"Your favorite cowboy is competin'. Don't tell me you don't want to watch."

Candy rolled her eyes and sipped her coffee as she watched Trudie load bean dip, shredded cheese, and everything else needed to construct a pile of nachos big enough to make all of Texas jealous. "Favorite cowboy, huh?"

Trudie looked over at her, one brow raised with a "that's a dumb question" expression on her face.

"Never mind." Candy rolled her eyes again.

Trudie was like a dog gnawing on a bone, and she wasn't gonna let it go until she got every detail about the time Candy had spent with Sterling.

"I'm gonna grab a shower." She gave Trudie a peck on the cheek and left the room.

She didn't want to say much about the whole experience, let alone how she felt about him leaving.

Trudie hadn't asked, but Candy knew better. It would come up somewhere between the heaping nachos and salted margaritas.

Candy unplugged her cell phone from the cord on the nightstand and took it into the bathroom with her.

No other messages had come from Sterling. Maybe he hadn't made it into the finals.

Sitting on the tub's edge, she debated what to send him. Praying she wouldn't be distracting in a bad way, she ran out and grabbed her purse.

When she was back in the bathroom, she stripped off her top.

Candy glossed her lips and unwrapped one of his lollipops. Arranging herself to get the angle right, she snapped the picture and sent it along with a message.

> Candy: Didn't want to distract you while you bowled, but I wanted you to know I was thinking of you all day and sending good luck vibes! I'm gonna assume you made the finals. So good luck tonight and know that you're on my mind.

Candy giggled, imagining his expression when he saw the shot of her.

Setting the phone by the sink, she took off the rest of her clothes and stepped into the shower.

Chapter Twenty-Nine

A MILLION TINY pins and needles tingled all over Sterling's right shoulder. He'd only meant to lie down and ice the thing for a bit.

Rubbing circles into the muscles, he tried to regain some blood flow, hoping there wasn't something more serious going on than just pain from overuse.

He glanced at the clock and was grateful there was still time to grab a bite to eat before checking in for the finals.

A quiet beep went off from his cell phone, and he pushed with his good arm to sit at the edge of the bed.

Rolling his stiff shoulder, he reached for his phone. He unlocked the screen and saw Candy had texted him back.

Holy hell!

Blinking his eyes quickly to clear his vision, he couldn't believe what she'd sent him. A pic of his Candy, her sexy eyes, pouty lips with one of his suckers in her mouth. And topless.

Well, it damn sure looked like she was topless. Just enough *not* showing to let his imagination run wild, and that it did.

Blood flowed in a rush to all the right places as he memorized every tiny detail of the picture in the message.

Forcing his mind from going everywhere his lips wanted to

be at that moment was a battle hard to fight, but he had to get to the alley, and soon.

He keyed in his reply.

> Sterling: Feisty filly! Good thing I'm not bowling right this minute cuz that was damn distracting! I loved it. Yes I did make the finals. All the wishes you're sending must be helping. I hope you're gonna be watching tonight.

Sterling walked into the bathroom to splash cold water on his face and had to adjust his erection in his jeans.

He thought hard of something to pull the image of Candy from the front of his mind.

A commercial he saw the other day came into focus, that one with all the puppies and the Sarah McLaughlin song. *Think of the puppies. Think of the puppies. Think of the... Whew.*

Taking a deep breath and letting it go as slowly as he could, he stopped and stared deep into the reflection of his blue eyes in the mirror. "This is it, cowboy. What you've been workin' so hard for. Let's git 'er done."

Sterling dried off, grabbed his gear, and headed for his destiny.

The parking lot overflowed with cars and people as he pulled in and found a space in the section reserved for the competitors.

It had been too long since he'd been in the middle of the circus frenzy these tournaments brought. He had missed it and longed to be back within it, but for the first time, it just didn't seem as exciting as it used to be.

Something was missing this time, and he had a feeling he knew what it was.

Pulling his bowling bag from the bed of the truck, he settled the strap over his good shoulder and, out of nervous habit, adjusted his hat.

He steeled his resolve and moved past the television network vans and on to the entrance.

Sterling swung open the glass door and froze, taking in the scene before him. The number of people milling around over-whelmed him more than he'd remembered.

Well, I'll be, guess it has been a while. He checked in and walked to the cordoned-off lanes dedicated for the final match competitors.

The onslaught of questions hollered to him from the media, coupled with the camera flashes, was harder to disregard this time, too.

"Sterling Day! How are you feeling tonight?" a female reporter called out.

"Mr. Day, did you ever think you would be competing in the finals again?" This time from a man.

"Sterling, can we get a quick interview with you?"

"How does it feel to be back?"

On and on it went. Trying not to let the attention rattle him, he ignored the machine gun full of questions being fired at him.

Thankfully, they couldn't enter the reserved area and get in any of the bowler's faces.

He focused on his custom blue and silver shoes, snugging them to his feet and tightening the laces. He stood and wiggled his toes, taking comfort in the familiarity.

Unable to stop himself, his gaze wandered over the crowd wrapped around the lanes. The lights were down over the sardine-like spectators, which helped them disappear into more of a dark haze.

Even the noise level had become nothing but a dull roar in his ears. *Damn, I need my candy.*

He fished a sucker out of his bowling bag, removed the wrapping, and popped it into his mouth.

The memory from their last night together flashed

through his mind, and he grinned at no one in particular. *Damn, I need* my *Candy.*

"How are ya? I'm Luke Williams. You must be Sterling Day." A short, balding man with a bad comb-over interrupted his thoughts and extended his hand. "I've heard a lot about you. It's a pleasure to be in the finals with you."

Sterling clasped the guy's hand in greeting. "Thanks, nice to meet ya. Should be a good game."

"When they told me I was rolling against you, I thought, 'No way.' I didn't even know he was still bowling. I mean…" Luke rambled on as Sterling only half paid attention. "I was still just coming up when you had your injury. Everyone said it was a career-ender, and yet here you are."

Does this guy ever stop talking? He's got enough tongue for ten rows of teeth.

"I can't wait to tell everyone back home how I beat Sterling Da—"

Sterling heard that last part loud and clear. "Wait just a damn minute. Game ain't even started yet, and *you* already won?" He sneered at the guy. "You best take a seat before you get the wrong end of this country boy."

"Well, if that's the way it's going to be, may the best man win," Luke replied with an arrogance Sterling could feel dripping off every word.

"That's the way it *is*, Luke. And I didn't come here to lose." Sterling leveled his stare at his opponent and crossed his arms.

Lil' bastard. It'd be a pleasure to teach his cocksure opponent a lesson in not counting his chickens before they hatched.

Sterling set out his towel and placed his ball in the return before sitting back down and pulling his wrist brace out of his bag. He snugged it to his arm and took another look around.

The crowd had started to settle down, and the spotlights intensified as the announcer's voice came over the loudspeakers, welcoming everyone to the final round of the Fort Worth PBA Tournament.

Sterling raised his hand and waved as they announced his name during the introduction of the competitors.

Past that, he couldn't hear anything else. He willed all the noises around him to silence as he got into focus.

He became the machine he needed to be. This was it. This was the real deal.

Chapter Thirty

CANDY SAT on the couch next to Trudie, each with a margarita in hand and a mountain of nachos on the coffee table in front of them.

Commercial after commercial played, giving airtime to every dang sponsor who'd given money to support the event.

A minor distraction as Sterling's text message went round and round in her mind. He was hoping she was watching. Damn straight, she'd be watching. Nothing short of a coma would keep her from it.

"You'd think we were watchin' the Superbowl with these commercials." Candy crunched a mouthful of corn chips.

Trudie snorted. "At least those are entertainin'."

"No kiddin'."

"You need a refill?"

Candy sat forward, focusing all her attention on the screen. "Hush now, tryin' to listen."

The two tournament announcers listed off the finalists competing, displaying headshots of both.

"There he is. Told you he made it," Trudie said.

"Luke Williams faces off with Sterling Day in tonight's event. It's

been quite some time since we've seen Sterling compete," the announcer said to his partner.

Candy jumped up, clapping, and let out a big yee-haw as if she were there and Sterling could hear her.

"Yes, Bob. In fact, it's been almost ten years since we last saw him in the circuit. Frankly, I'm—"

Trudie muted the TV. "Whoa, darlin', that's a whole lotta excitement for someone you keep denying." She narrowed her eyes. "What aren't you telling me, Candy?"

"Wha—" Candy plopped back down in her seat. "Don't know what you're talkin' about, Trudie. And turn the sound back on, will ya? I wanna hear what they're sayin'." She grabbed her drink and drained the last of it in one gulp. "Hey, I need a refill."

"How much 'datin'' did you two do exactly?"

"Okay, fine. I'll get the drinks."

"Candy Jameson!" She trailed Candy into the kitchen. "You rode that boy like a wild bronco, didn't you?"

"What? Good God, Trudie. We spent some time together, is all." She tried for all it was worth to compose her face but couldn't keep the grin from parting her lips. It was getting too hard to hold it all in, though.

"It's about time." Trudie grabbed the mix from the fridge, looking quite pleased with herself.

"I said we spent some time, nothin' more." Candy frowned and measured out the tequila. "I don't want the whole town knowin', so you best zip them hot pink lips of yours."

"Scout's honor." Trudie made the three-fingered sign. "Come on now, give me every dirty detail." She mixed their drinks in the shaker.

Candy scoffed at her friend and then crossed her arms. "You didn't do a very good job before."

"I said I was sorry about that. You forgave me. Besides, look at you." Trudie poured two fresh margaritas. "You're 'bout ready to burst, you wanna tell so bad."

Candy sighed, palmed her cell phone from the counter, and reread his message. She'd left it in the kitchen for this very reason, so she wouldn't keep reading and rereading it.

She looked up at her friend. "The only thing I'm gonna tell you is we saw each other a lot…oh, and lane ten will never be the same again." She chuckled, set the phone back down, grabbed her drink, and went to the couch to watch.

Screw it. He was gone, and the whole town already knew they'd been dating. They'd never believe she actually had sex with him inside Bowling Dreams, let alone on one of the lanes.

Trudie gaped after her, drink in hand, then joined her on the couch. "You're pullin' my leg. You really sexed the boy up on the actual lane? When?"

Candy bit into a chip, chewed and swallowed. Drawing out the moment, she took a long sip of her drink. Making Trudie sweat was too fun. "Never you mind when." She tilted her head to the side. "Set the foul buzzer off a time or two."

"Well, I'll be." Trudie gulped her drink. "You done me proud."

"Only you would say that. Ooh, look, they're about to start."

"Was he good?"

"Trudie!"

"Spill! I gotta know." Trudie shimmied her hips on the sofa.

Candy sat back and let out a resigned sigh. She looked at Trudie and back at the TV. "Best I ever had."

Trudie slapped Candy's knee. "Yee-haw!"

"Ouch!" Candy rubbed the spot Trudie'd struck. "Can we watch now?"

"Yes, ma'am." Trudie sat back, smiling.

They watched in silence as Luke Williams started, then cheered when Sterling took his turn.

They were neck and neck the whole game, and she

cringed when she watched Sterling rub his shoulder as the game wore on. *Dang, he's gettin' sore.*

"Lookin' like his shoulder's givin' him trouble," Trudie said.

"I hope it holds for him. He's worked so hard to get back in this very position."

They were down to the last few rounds, and Candy found herself torn between knowing if he won, she'd probably never see him again, and if he lost, maybe she would.

A twinge of guilt rang through her at the latter. She wanted him to win. But she also didn't want to let him go.

Sterling held her heart in his hands, though she'd never intended on putting it there. It'd happened just the same, and now...now she had no idea what would happen.

"This is it. Final ball of the tenth frame." Trudie gripped Candy's arm, dragging her from her thoughts.

Candy sat forward, and they both fell silent. If Sterling rolled a strike, he'd take the win.

He lowered his head and began his approach. The ball flew, and Sterling held his position, arm high in the air. The swirling ball hugged the edge and made its turn into the pocket— STRIKE!

"Woo-hoo!" Trudie jumped up from the couch.

Candy jumped up, too, clapping her hands and cheering. Her cheeks dampened as she realized she'd started crying.

He'd done it, and she was so dang proud of him.

Question was, were these happy or sad tears? She couldn't tell, but one thing was for sure—she'd probably just lost her cowboy.

The realization settled heavily in her mind and heart. She didn't want to lose him. He was everything she never knew she wanted. And now he was gone.

Chapter Thirty-One

STERLING SHATTERED HIS LAST FRAME, not a pin standing, and cinched his seat back with the pros.

The crowd roared to its feet, and he released a relieved breath he hadn't known he'd been holding in.

He locked eyes with his arrogant opponent as he removed his wrist brace and then extended his hand as he walked toward him to thank him for a good game.

"Guess you were right," Luke said, barely audible over the crowd.

"Been a long time comin'." Sterling refrained from gloating. *Momma always told me to be a good sport.*

"Congratulations, you definitely earned it." Luke withdrew his hand and rubbed the back of his neck. "I'll be back next year. Count on it."

"Wouldn't expect anythin' less."

Sterling returned to his bag and dropped his wrist brace in its pocket before grabbing his hat.

TV reporters from the many stations covering the event jockeyed for position around him after the officials dropped the barriers keeping the crowd out.

Blood pounded through his veins as he drank in all the

excitement. The pride of accomplishment filled him, yet hollowness also tugged hard within him.

One of the two main announcers for the event broke through the myriad of interviewers and rescued Sterling from the avalanche of interest in him.

He placed his hand on Sterling's arm. "If you'll come with me to the winner's podium, Mr. Day." He gestured to their destination. "I think you'll find it better suited to answer all these questions."

Sterling let the man lead him away. A pretty, young blonde met him as he stepped up to the center of the stage. She held a large trophy shining almost as bright as the flashes in the room.

This could only be better if Candy were the one bringing him his prize.

He accepted the large golden cup and paused for the obligatory photos snapping around him. He stepped forward and set it on a small table to the left of the podium strewn with microphones.

The crowd quieted as Sterling adjusted his hat to deflect some of the glare from the hot lights targeting him. "Bet y'all didn't expect to see me again." He chuckled and flashed his practiced prize-winning grin.

The crowd howled in unison and applauded before quieting again. Then, a rumble of unintelligible questions built before one broke through the charge, loud and clear.

"Sterling Day, no one expected to see you attempt a come-back. How does it feel to be here once more?" a handsome middle-aged man in a tailored suit asked.

"Well, I gotta admit it feels darn good." Sterling paused. "But I made up my mind and trained hard for this. I knew what I wanted and wasn't gonna accept any less."

More applause from the crowd.

"Many said your injury nearly a decade ago was a career-ender. What made you think otherwise?" a different reporter's voice came through as the noise level subsided.

"I worked with a great physical therapist." He adjusted his hat. "I guess I wouldn't take no for an answer, and he believed in my drive to be on top once more."

"Anything you'd like to attribute your win to today?" another voice from the crowd asked.

Sterling paused in thought, then pulled a sucker from his shirt pocket. "I couldn't have done it today without my Candy."

He winked into one of the many TV cameras and held out his lollipop. Nothing could be truer. Candy made the last month better than he'd ever dreamed possible.

The crowd cheered louder as the reporters started shouting more questions.

"Candy, Mr. Day? Care to elaborate?"

"Do you always have suckers when you bowl?"

"Is candy your good luck charm?"

Sterling's chest filled with pride. *Damn right she is!*

"Are you sponsored by a candy company?"

"No more questions for now, y'all. I appreciate all the attention, but you should save some for when I win Vegas."

The cheers from the crowd rose and drowned out the reporters. Sterling held his trophy in the air, and camera flashes lit up the space like the Fourth of July.

After another moment, he stepped off the stage and moved to the private section in the back of the building. Someone had been gracious enough to bring all his gear and boots and have them waiting for him.

A woman in a well-pressed business suit and glasses approached him, introducing herself as Ms. Brewster. She congratulated him, then started rattling off his itinerary for the next day.

Sterling only half listened as his thoughts raced through

his mind like a Texas twister. *Screw you, Mr. Mechanical Bull. I showed your ass!*

CANDY WIPED the tears from her cheeks, hoping Trudie didn't see, as Sterling accepted his trophy and stepped onto the podium to answer questions.

"Look how cute he is," Trudie said. "Almost ten years? My word, how old is he?"

Candy shifted on the couch and swallowed past the lump in her throat. "You don't remember him from before he was on the circuit? I kinda figured you did."

"I wasn't payin' attention to bowlin' ten years ago, sugar. Too busy chasin' a bull rider across Oklahoma." She paused, a spark lighting in her eyes. "He had impressive thighs, bigger than my waist around, among other things." Trudie sipped her drink.

"You really can't have a conversation without bringing sex into it or the size of a man's penis, can you?"

"Hell, no. Life's just too short not to enjoy the fruits of God's labor." Trudie brushed a piece of lint off her leg. "So, how old is Sterling?"

"I don't know exactly. Older than me, I'm guessin'." She sighed and stared blankly at the television. "We never discussed age; talked about lots of other stuff, but not age."

"Sounds sweet; dating and pillow talk can be nice."

"I couldn't have done it today without my Candy."

Candy wanted to downplay the "dating and pillow talk" Trudie was swooning about when Sterling's comment stopped her short.

She focused her attention on the TV. Looking straight into the camera, he held out a lollipop and winked. *He didn't just—*

"I'll be damned! He's talkin' 'bout you, Candy."

"Nah, no, he isn't." Candy's heart pounded in her ears, beating with a rhythm of hope.

She jumped to her feet, grabbed the now-empty nacho plate and headed to the kitchen.

Hope was a dangerous emotion to have.

"He was. How can you think he wasn't?" Trudie followed with their empty glasses in hand. "That comment was more obvious than a nun in a whorehouse."

"A what?" Candy shook her head and started washing the dishes.

"Never mind. Call him." Trudie set her glass beside the sink. "You should call him, honey."

"He's busy. You saw for yourself." Candy shrugged, mentally trying to pull back on her emotions. She felt like a runaway train. "I'll send him a congratulations text later."

"At the very least, you should see if he's gonna roll back through town on his way out. I know I would." Trudie leaned in and kissed Candy on the cheek. "Gotta run, sugar, Billy's probably home by now. I'll see you Tuesday at work."

"Yes, ma'am. Thanks for bringing the goodies by and watchin' the tourney with me." Candy grabbed the dish towel to dry her hands and walked her friend to the door. "I had fun."

"Me, too, doll. Be good now, and if ya can't, then be good at it." Trudie stepped out the door.

Though it was forced, Candy laughed and leaned against the doorjamb as she watched her friend get in her car and pull away.

Could he have been talking about her with his little comment about candy? She supposed it was possible. He'd told her he missed his "Candy."

But being the simple girl she was, Candy sure as heck didn't want to be a fool and read anything into it.

After all, the man sucked on those Dum-Dums like they

were going out of style. It was his thing, one of the tools of his game.

Candy finished washing the dishes and cleaned up the remains of their watch party. With the task complete, she grabbed her cell and sat at the kitchen table.

Not expecting a message in return, she sent one, and *only* one, telling him congratulations. She meant it, too. She was happy for him.

Changing into a set of comfy pajamas, Candy curled up on the couch with her nana's afghan and her latest cross-stitch she'd been neglecting and listened to whatever she could find on TV good enough to be distracting.

Sterling Day was something special for sure. And as she tamped down the little flutters of hope that insisted on rising inside her mind, she resigned herself to the fact that she'd most likely never see him again.

Life would return to normal, and it would all feel like a dream as time passed.

Wouldn't it?

She'd had her chance at her dream. She'd tasted and touched it. But now it was gone, no longer within reach.

Lord, this just plain sucked.

This was a horrible joke. Just like she thought when this started with him.

Grief and despair took up residence in her mind. Shaking her head, she buried her face in her hands and let the tears come.

Chapter Thirty-Two

STERLING AWOKE with a start on Monday morning to the sound of the hotel phone ringing. A wake-up call he didn't remember requesting.

He hung the phone back on its cradle and rubbed the sleep from his eyes.

Not for the first time, he found himself grateful he'd stopped drinking all those years back. All the excitement from yesterday's win had him plum-tuckered out, and he'd slept like the dead.

The reality of achieving his goal just began to scratch the surface. *Holy hell! I won!*

As he rolled himself to the edge of the bed and sat up, he reached for his cell phone to check for messages. There was only one he really wanted to see

Candy had texted, and he'd missed it during all the commotion.

Candy: Congratulations!!!

She did *watch me play.* Excitement rolled through him, like he'd become a high school kid who found out his crush might like him back.

His cheeks were starting to ache from the grin taking up residence on his face.

Sterling set the phone down and started for the bathroom. He needed to get cleaned up and moving based on Ms. Brewster's description of all he needed to do.

Meetings with sponsors, a photo shoot, two separate interviews, and lunch with the tournament hosts, to name a few.

He planned on texting Candy later when he had a break. Right then, he had to mobilize before things got too overwhelming.

Ms. Brewster picked him up promptly at eight that morning, and as soon as he opened his hotel room door, she began rattling off the agenda for the day.

She was pure efficiency, from her sensible shoes and dark gray suit to her hair pulled back in a tight bun.

He bet she had at least two pencils hiding in her hair somewhere.

The woman had been all about business from the moment she introduced herself right down to insisting they take her car as she rushed him out the door.

"Any chance of breakfast?" Sterling took a seat inside her black Lincoln Town Car.

She settled in the driver's seat. "Not really in the schedule. I believe they will have a buffet at the photo shoot." She started the car and pulled out of the parking lot.

"And is that before or after the first interview?"

"After. We have you scheduled for the interview with Bowlers Journal first thing, then pictures to follow," she said.

"As long as they don't mind my stomach tryin' to answer the questions for me."

"Don't worry, Mr. Day, I'll try to make this as painless as possible for you."

Sterling was out of practice with the publicity machine

and grateful he had a guide, however stuffy she might be, to get him on his way.

"All right, just do me a favor and call me Sterling." He popped one of his cherished suckers in his mouth. "I keep thinking my dad is in the car when you say 'Mr. Day.'"

She nodded but said nothing more.

The day flew by like a racing Thoroughbred. Interview after interview, his eyes still held a blurred spot from the abundance of flashbulbs.

"Over here, Mr. Day." "Hold up the trophy, Mr. Day." "Can you do that again?" "This time, hold up the sucker."

After the first stop on the list, Sterling realized his cell phone wasn't with him. He cursed himself for not replying to Candy when he'd had the chance this morning.

Hell, considering how crazy the day had been, he wouldn't have had time to reply to her anyway.

Sterling declined the invitation for one last meeting over dinner, citing exhaustion as the cause. At least he wasn't lying.

Ms. Brewster dropped him off at the entrance to his hotel with one last congratulations and a handshake.

He tipped his hat to her and turned to drag his two-ton boots toward the elevators.

After closing and locking the door behind him, he set his hat on the counter and fell on his bed like a bag of dirty laundry. *Boots, cowboy. Don't fall asleep in your boots.*

He muscled himself upright and let his boots fall to the floor. Picking his phone up, he checked to see if any new messages had come in while he was away.

There was none. He couldn't blame her.

Not wanting to feel like any more of an ass than he already did, he punched in a quick message before the sandman got a death grip on him and dragged him off to Dreamland.

Sterling: Exhausted. Gonna pass out.

With his last ounce of energy, he stripped down to his birthday suit and crawled between the sheets.

CANDY WAITED all last night to hear back from Sterling. And then, she waited all day today, too. She was about to go out of her mind pacing her trailer, completely out of things to do, when she'd gotten called into work that evening.

She leaned against the front counter, pulled her phone from her back pocket, and looked at the screen.

Nothing. Not one stinking thing.

No "thank you," no "how're you?"

If she checked her phone even one more time and found nothing, she might bowl the dang thing down lane ten and say to hell with Sterling Day.

With men altogether, for that matter.

She sure as heck wasn't waiting another cotton pickin' minute more.

With a grunt, she walked into the office, stuffed her phone in her purse and decided leaving it there might be best for the night. Maybe even until morning.

The man was long gone, that was for dang sure, and she'd just have to accept that.

So what if they'd had a great time on their dates? So what if the sex was incredible? So what if he'd taken an interest in her and her life?

So what if he'd made love to her into the early morning hours the night before he'd left, touching her in ways no one had ever touched her?

And so what if something had burst to life inside her in the short time they'd been together? Something that made her long for more…long to see if there had been at least a chance of more?

So. What.

Candy returned to the front desk and pinched the bridge of her nose. Her head was throbbing.

Damn! Damn! Dammit! To hell with her stupid expectations. To hell with her silly dreams.

This was real life she was living in, and she needed to remember that.

"Hey there, darlin'." Trudie approached her, carrying two beers in her hands. "You look like you need one of these."

Candy eyed the clock, almost closing time. Screw it. "Thanks, I do." She took the offered beer and downed a long swig.

"You talk to him, hear from him?"

"Nope." Candy wiped her mouth with the back of her hand. "Didn't figure I would, though." She shrugged and tipped the bottle back again.

"Baby girl, you got caught up, didn't you?" Trudie pursed her lips and rubbed Candy's hand. "It happens to the best of us, precious."

"Can we not talk about it? I don't want to talk about it."

"We never have to talk about it again." Trudie squeezed her hand.

Candy took another swig of her beer. "It's just…I thought, ya know?" She shook her head. "We only spent a month together, but it was the best month I've ever had. And…" She picked at the label on the side of the bottle. "No one's ever seemed so interested in me before. I mean, really in *me*, ya know?" She tipped the bottle back, then set it down again. "It ain't like he was tryin' to get in my pants by talkin' all sweet and stuff. I'd already given it up to him. A *bunch*." Candy cringed, then shook her head and waved her hand in front of her face. "I really don't want to talk about this, Trudie!"

"All right, honey. You don't have to." Trudie rested her elbows on the counter.

"I guess I just hoped." She dropped her head. "I'm silly. I shoulda known better." She looked at Trudie, feeling the tears begin to well up. "Why am I so upset?" She swiped at her eyes. "I don't wanna be this upset."

Trudie ran around the counter, pulled Candy into the back office, and hugged her.

"Shh," Trudie crooned, stroking Candy's hair. "It's okay, baby girl."

"I don't want to talk about this, Trudie!" Candy cried and buried her face in her friend's shoulder.

"Yes, you said that." Trudie pulled away after a few minutes, grabbed a tissue, and handed it to Candy. "G'on in the bathroom and clean yourself up now."

"Okay." Candy turned, tears still falling, and sniffled. "Thanks, Trudie," she whispered, then disappeared into the small office powder room.

"Sure thing, sugar. I'm heading back out to the bar."

Candy wiped her mascara-stained cheeks and blew her nose. She stared at her reflection briefly, muttered a curse, and stepped back into the office.

On her way out, she heard the faint beep of her cell. She stopped dead in her tracks and listened again.

Beep.

She darted back toward the desk, ripped her purse open, and dug for the phone. *Desperate much?* Finding it, she pulled it out and flipped it open.

Sterling: Exhausted. Gonna pass out.

She plopped down into the desk chair and reread the message. It was different compared to the other messages he'd sent.

She stared at the phone, debating whether or not to text him back.

Shaking her head at her foolishness, she closed the phone and stuffed it back in her purse.

No, she might be feeling a little heartbroken, which was stupid considering the circumstances, but she wasn't anyone's sucker.

Candy finished her beer and went on about her closing duties. Finally done, she got her things together and headed for home.

When she'd settled herself in bed, she stared at the text from Sterling again, and in a moment of tired weakness, she sent off one final text to him.

> Candy: No worries, cowboy. You're busy. It was nice while it lasted. Wishing you all the best going forward. Take care.

With a sigh, she closed her phone.

After setting it on the nightstand, Candy curled herself around her pillows.

She hadn't felt this depressed since Jared left, and she realized he wasn't coming back. And still, this felt worse.

Thank God for sleep. Sleep would be her savior because this was just too much to bear.

Chapter Thirty-Three

STERLING PRESSED his good arm against the shower wall and let the warm water wash over his body.

Every bit of exertion from the weekend came back to haunt him with a vengeance. And this morning, it was winning.

Straightening, he rubbed his bad shoulder and then attempted to lift his arm with little success.

He tried to convince himself it was muscle fatigue, much like returning to the gym after a long hiatus—the second day was always the killer.

Tough it out, and get back to the gym. If not, couch potato was the new plan.

He rubbed stronger circles into the muscle, willing the blood to flow and bring him back some mobility. A little ice and some ibuprofen ought to do the trick.

His arm started moving, weak but moving. Damn thing hurt like hell—no way he could deny that.

With a towel secured around his waist, he stepped from the bathroom and got dressed.

A faint beep came from the dresser, and without thinking, he jerked his arm toward the cell that lay there.

Shit! That frickin' hurt. But…hell yeah, his arm moved!

Clenching his teeth, he pulled his right arm tight to his body and took a deep breath before reaching for his phone with his other arm.

Thank God there was a month until Vegas.

A new message from Candy showed on his screen.

Excitement pulsed through him…until he read it.

Cowboy? Nice while it lasted? Take care?

What was that all about? Was she brushing him off?

He scrolled up to his last message to her. *Aww shiiiit.* Sterling closed his eyes and let his head slump with a big sigh.

He'd been so tired when he sent it he wasn't even thinking straight. The text had been damned impersonal compared to the others he'd sent prior. It was no wonder she'd replied like she had.

Screw this texting shit. He always took things head-on, and this shouldn't be any different.

The publicity machine was done for now. He needed to get his denim-covered ass back home, rest his shoulder, and prepare for Vegas.

And God help him, pick up his favorite Candy along the way.

So no texting back; he'd screwed that up. He wasn't calling her either. The next conversation with her was going to be face-to-face.

It was noon before he checked out of the hotel with his suitcase and bowling bag loaded into the bed of his F-150.

He promised to stop by the bowling alley before leaving town to sign a few posters.

His shoulder pain had barely let up, and his stomach grumbled, reminding him he hadn't eaten yet. But he ignored it. If he got done at the alley and back behind the wheel by one, two o'clock at the latest, he'd be in Strawn by three or four. *Maybe I'll catch her before she heads to work.*

. . .

STOPPING ONLY for food and gas, he kept straightaway on the highway. His truck chewed up the miles with ease, and it wasn't long before the exit sign for Strawn came into view.

Turning off the highway, he drove north as the large billboard caught his attention again.

Welcome to Strawn, Texas.
Home of The National Bowling Champion
Mason Jennings

Sterling chuckled. "Can't imagine Las Cruces will be doing that for me anytime soon."

He turned the corner to her little mobile home park and pulled up in front of her trailer. Her car was gone. Damn, maybe she was already at work.

Sterling backed up and headed in that direction, keeping his eyes peeled as he drove by the few shopping plazas along the way, just in case she was there.

As he approached Bowling Dreams and pulled in, he spotted the tail end of Candy's car parked next to the building.

Hoping she would let him explain, he parked his car, got out, and placed his hat on his head.

It was time to either make things right or go home having tried.

Sterling rubbed his sore shoulder as he entered and saw the place busy with the after-work crowd. Mason stood behind the counter, but Candy was nowhere in sight.

He peered down to the far end of the lanes—still no sight of her. When he turned, Trudie, looking sassy as ever with a new pink strip dyed in her hair, stood before him, hands on her hips.

"Well, look what the cat dragged in." She looked him up and down. "Congrats on the win, sugar."

"Thanks, Trudie, you got to watch, huh?"

"Yup, watched the whole thang. Didn't think we'd be seein' you back in these parts anytime soon." She popped her gum and pursed her lips. "What can I get ya? A lane, a drink, or maybe some Candy?"

Sterling took a step back and popped his thumbs in his jeans pockets. "Now that you mention it, you seen Candy? I was hoping to find her here tonight."

"What's it worth to ya?" Trudie narrowed her eyes at him. "I'm not much on you big-city boys comin' round here and breakin' my girl's heart."

"If that were the case, I wouldn't even be here." He cocked his head to the side, appreciating her protectiveness over Candy. "Feel like helpin' out an old pro?"

"All right, cowboy." She sighed. "I guess you have a point. Last time I checked, she was in the pinsetting area behind the lanes, getting Joe to actually do some work."

"Thanks, Trudie." He tipped his hat in appreciation and stepped around her.

"Good luck, sugar," she hollered after him.

Sterling waved in thanks and made a beeline to where she directed him.

His stomach started knotting up. What if she didn't want anything to do with him? *Man up, cowboy.* He knew what he wanted. He just needed to go get her.

He made his way through the door to the back. If he thought the bowling area seemed loud, it was nothing compared to the close confines of the pinsetting machines and the constant echoes of crashing balls and pins.

Candy stood just ahead with her back to him, talking to who he assumed had to be Joe.

Eyes locked on his target, Sterling moved in her direction.

Apparently done with her conversation, she turned around and stopped dead in her tracks when she spotted him.

Chapter Thirty-Four

Candy blinked, then blinked again, convinced she was imagining things.

Sterling approached her with such a determined look in his eyes that she took a step back.

Before she could make heads or tails of what was happening, he grabbed her, pulled her against his lean, muscled chest, and, with his fingers tangled in her hair, planted a deep kiss on her lips.

She stiffened but quickly gave in to the heat of his body surrounding her and opened for him. He groaned and deepened the kiss further, his mouth urgent and possessive.

As the taste and feel of him penetrated, a blazing inferno raced through her entire body, searing her from head to toe and thawing the thin ice she'd formed around her heart toward him.

With all that she felt, she was helpless to deny him. Candy melted against him, her hands shaking and clinging to his shoulders.

Sweet Lord, he felt like heaven on earth.

When Sterling pulled away, they were both breathing

heavy. He pressed her head to his chest and stroked her hair. "I'm so fucking sorry."

Candy closed her eyes and listened to his heartbeat and heavy breaths—too frightened to give life to what she might have felt in his kiss. She willed her own rapid heart to calm.

When she could finally speak, she lifted her head and met his gaze. "What are you doing here?"

"I had to see you. We need to talk." He stroked her cheek. "God, you're beautiful."

Candy felt the blush tingle in her cheeks and lowered her lashes at his sweet compliment.

Joe coughed. "I'll leave you two alone." He scooted past them toward the exit.

"I missed you. I missed you more than I've ever missed anyone, and considerin' I've never really had anyone to miss before, I figure that's a pretty big deal."

"Come with me." She pulled him into a nearby storeroom away from the noise of the machines and closed the door behind them.

"I'm sorry about my text message," he said when she turned to face him. "Look." He set his hat on a stack of boxes and ran his palm over his short hair. "I'm not very good at this, but I can do better. You deserve better."

"You don't owe me anything. We had a good time. That's all. I don't expect more." She wrapped her arms around her middle. "It's okay, Sterling. Really, it is."

"Okay, but what if I want more?"

"Now you're talkin' crazy. We've only known each other a month."

"That's the thing. I felt somethin' with you." He shook his head. "Did you feel anythin'?" He sat down on an overturned crate. "Shit, am I makin' a fool of myself here?"

Candy leaned against the door, hope rising inside her heart despite her efforts to keep it roped down. "No, you're not makin' a fool of yourself. I felt it, too." She avoided his gaze and held herself still, trying to keep some form of control over her swirling emotions.

"I won, ya know? I worked so hard to get ready to win that damn tournament." He stood and started pacing the small space. "It's all I've thought about for years."

"You earned it. I'm—"

"No, let me finish, please. I need to tell you this."

"Okay. Go on." She stepped away from the door and sat on the crate he'd vacated.

"The whole time I was there, round after round, win after win, I felt incredible, and then at night, when it was quiet, it wasn't enough. I'd get in bed alone and read a little message from you, and all I could think about was how much I wanted you there with me. And that's crazy, right?" He rubbed the back of his neck. "Because like you said, we only spent a short time together, but regardless of how short a time I've known you, I felt it anyway. I couldn't shake it, and it became all I could think about." He stopped pacing and faced her.

Candy's mind spun in circles as she tried to track the words he was saying. He talked so fast and paced in front of her like some sort of caged animal. He couldn't possibly mean what she thought he was saying to her, could he?

"Sterling. I—"

"I couldn't recognize it for what it was, but I get it now. It was wrong because you weren't there. This victory...this opportunity means nothing now if I can't have you there to share it with." He stepped closer. "I'm in love with you, Candy. I'm asking you to come with me. Will you come with me?"

He what? She jumped up. "Are you nuts?"

"Maybe."

"I've got a job, responsibilities, a huge debt to pay." Now, it was her turn to pace. Sure, she loved him, too, but that didn't mean she should run off with him. How was that any different than what she'd done with Jared?

"You hate it here. You told me that yourself."

"Yeah, but that doesn't change the fact that this is the hand that life dealt me." What in the heck was he trying to do to her? Good Lord, her heart raced a mile a minute at the idea he was laying out. Could this really be happening?

"Candy, look at me."

She stopped moving but kept her back to him. Her body trembled with nervous tension, and she clenched her hands at her sides. "I'm scared," she whispered.

Candy felt more than heard him move behind her. His warmth rolled over her, sending bursts of electricity dancing over her already sensitive skin.

Sterling snaked his arms around her waist and pulled her back against his front.

She released the breath she didn't realize she was holding, wrapped her arms around his, and let her head fall back against his chest. "I'm scared, Sterling."

"So am I."

"What if we find out it doesn't work between us?"

"What if we find out it does?"

Everything inside her went soft. God, this man! "Sweet Jesus, where did you come from?"

"Las Cruces." He chuckled and nuzzled her neck. "Come home with me. I want to love you every night in my bed." He kissed her shoulder. "I want to wake up next to you every mornin'." He turned her to face him. "And I want to win that tournament with you by my side." He kissed her lips. "Even if I don't win it, it won't matter because I'll still have you."

Candy rose on tiptoe and wrapped her arms around his neck. "You're crazy, you know that?"

"You may be right, but I'm okay with that." He winced as he picked her up and kissed her again.

She wrapped her legs around his waist and matched the rub of his tongue with her own—a fevered kiss laced with the promise of a new future, a new beginning.

Screw Jared, and screw her past. This was nothing like that. She was older, wiser and she'd be crazy to give Sterling up.

"Yes," she said against his lips.

He pulled back and gave her a soft, sexy grin. "Yes?"

She rolled her lips between her teeth and nodded.

"Candy Jameson, does that mean love me, too?"

She shook her head and pressed her forehead to his. "Sterling Day, as crazy as it sounds, yes, that's exactly what it means. I am one hundred percent in love with you."

"Yeow!" He gripped her ass and hiked her up higher on his waist.

A squeal burst out of her at his excitement. "You're probably gonna regret this in a matter of days, ya know."

"Doubt it." He strode for the door. "Though I make no promises that you won't wanna kill me. I've been told I'm a huge pain in the ass."

She laughed. "You can put me down now. I saw that wince. I know your shoulder must be sore, honey."

"Hush, I like you just where you are."

"Well, then. If isn't this all *Officer and a Gentleman* like, I don't know what is," she said. "Hey, where's your hat? I should wear it while you whisk me away to our happy ever after."

"Oh damn, see what you do to me? Almost forgot my hat." He located it and leaned forward with her still in his arms. "G'on, scoop it up and place it on that gorgeous head of yours."

Candy grabbed the hat and did as he said. She locked her ankles around his lower back and held tight to his shoulders while he made his way down the concrete walkway next to the lanes toward the exit.

Hiking herself up further, she pulled the hat off her head as they neared the open area and waved it in the air above them as she bounced in his arms. "Giddy-up, cowboy!"

He gripped her ass tighter. "Keep bouncin' like that, and we'll never make it outta here."

Trudie stood in the hall holding Candy's purse, grinning and clapping, when she spotted them approaching.

"Way to go, Candy! Way to go!" Trudie shouted and clapped. Quoting the very movie Candy had just teased Sterling about.

"Okay, put me down now. That was just a little far beyond corny." She rubbed his shoulder, and Sterling released his hold, letting her slide down his tall body.

She gave him his hat and a quick peck on his sweet lips, then turned toward Trudie. "You knew, didn't you?" She took her purse from her friend's hands.

"I had a feelin'."

"Will you come visit?"

"Of course, sweetheart." Trudie pulled her into an embrace. "You're gonna be happy, honey. I know it," she whispered.

"I love you, Trudie." She kissed her cheek.

"I love you too, sugar. Now get on outta here. I'll worry about gettin' your car home for you."

"Thanks. Tell Joe and Mason goodbye for me, too?"

"'Course I will." Trudie cupped Candy's cheek in her palm. To Sterling, she said, "You take care of my girl."

"Wouldn't have it any other way." He tipped his hat and then looked down at Candy. "You ready?"

"As ready as I'll ever be."

He reached for her hand, and she took it. She laced her fingers with his, and they headed for the door.

The sun had just started to set as they walked across the parking lot.

Shades of pink and gold spread across the broad Texas sky in front of them, and wildflowers from the open field across the street filled the air with sweetness, making everything smell new and fresh.

It all felt like one of those happy endings in Hollywood movies.

"We need to go get my clothes," she said.

"Clothes? You mean you're not gonna be walkin' around buck nekkid for me?"

"Oh Lord, you need some home trainin', don't you?"

"Sugar, you can train me all you want." He swatted her backside.

Candy yelped and rubbed her butt cheek, then rewarded him with a devilish grin.

"We'll grab some clothes and figure out how to get the rest of your stuff later."

"Already got this all worked out, huh?"

"Nah." He unlocked her door and opened it for her. "I'm flyin' blind here. How'm I doin' so far?"

"Pretty darn good." She turned and kissed him before dropping into the passenger seat.

When Sterling settled in the driver's seat beside her, she looked at him, taking in his profile: his straight nose, full lips, and strong chin.

"You okay, darlin'?"

"Yep. Just appreciatin' my knight in shining bowling shoes."

"Well, damn. If I'm a knight, then that makes you my princess. Hey, we might need a nicer carriage." He grinned and started the car. "But at least this one doesn't turn into a pumpkin after midnight."

"Ooh, clever! Must be that new Candy you got yourself." She nudged his side as they drove away from Bowling Dreams.

As Candy looked back at the neon sign, hope rose in her heart for the first time in a long time.

Things would be different now, and even if it didn't turn out perfect, she planned to enjoy every minute of it.

She turned around, leaned her head on Sterling's shoulder, and looked forward, determined never to look back again.

Dorothy F. Shaw & T. D. Hoffman

About the Authors
Dorothy F. Shaw & T.D. Hoffman

Dorothy F. Shaw

Dorothy F. Shaw lives in Arizona, where the weather is hot, and the sunsets are always beautiful. She's a self-proclaimed sex scene snob and is proud of it. When she's not writing, she's thinking about writing.

With her ever-open heart, bright red hair, and many colorful tattoos, she truly lives and loves in Technicolor!

Get in bed (and read) with your favorite redhead!

Newsletter sign-up: Yes, please!
Join *Dorothy's Ruby Readers* on FB:
http://bit.ly/DFSRubyReaders
www.dorothyfshaw.com
DorothyFShaw@Gmail.com

facebook.com/AuthorDorothyFShaw

instagram.com/authordorothyfshaw

bsky.app/profile/dorothyfshaw.bsky.social

tiktok.com/@authordorothyfshaw

threads.net/@authordorothyfshaw

goodreads.com/dorothyfshaw

amazon.com/stores/author/B00DPRI5HK

bookbub.com/profile/dorothy-f-shaw

T.D. Hoffman

T.D. Hoffman is a man of many talents. Not only is he an award-winning tattoo artist, known in the tattoo community as Wookie, he's also a biker as well as a dedicated father of four.

Unafraid to try new things, T.D. simply decided he wanted to write a novel, and so it began from there.

T.D. welcomes e-mails at: WookieStyleAZ@gmail.com

You can also find him on his FB fan page Facebook.com/WookieStyleArt or his website for his shop: https://www.wookiestyleaz.com/

Also by Dorothy F. Shaw

Head to my site to find all links to my available backlist:
www.DorothyFShaw.com

Dorothy F. Shaw & T.D. Hoffman
Phoenix, Arizona
SPARE HEARTS
Copyright © 2025 by Dorothy F. Shaw & T.D. Hoffman
ISBN-10: 0-9978310-5-7
ISBN-13: 978-0-9978310-5-4
Edited by: Lauren Plude
Cover by: Scott Carpenter

Red Queen Publications electronic publication: April 2025

Publishing History

Digital 1.0 edition / August 2013

Digital/Print 2.0 edition / April 2025

Red Queen
Publications